COLUMBUS CREATIVE COOPERATIVE

ORIGINS

AN ANTHOLOGY

This anthology is proudly sponsored by

Sunny Meadows
Flower Farm

www.OurSunnyMeadows.com

Pauquette ltd
dba Columbus Creative Cooperative
1658 Harvard Ave.
Columbus, OH 43203
www.ColumbusCoop.org

EDITOR
Kim Younkin

PRODUCTION EDITOR
Brad Pauquette

PROOFREADER
Mallory Baker

Cover photograph by Melissa Pauquette, 2009.
Printed with permission.
MelissaPauquettePhotography.com

ISBN 978-0-9835205-0-4

Printed in the United States of America
1 3 5 7 9 10 8 6 4 2

CONTENTS

INTRODUCTION

It's a bad idea to check your phone while sitting on the commode. There are just too many things that can go wrong.

The accidental picture message, the inadvertent call answering, "Hello, excuse the echo," and lest we forget—the inevitable bobble, fumble and ultimate plunge into the murky depths below.

Plop.

I think you'll find in the pages that follow a suitable substitute for those minutes of your day spent waiting on a city bus, staring out the window while the server fetches your lunch, delaying the walk into work, or avoiding the temptation to check your phone… however you're indisposed.

The nine short stories that follow are a collection of fantastic work from local Columbus writers. These are stories written by your waitress, your kid's tutor, your receptionist and your attorney, all of whom have devoted a tremendous amount of time to practicing the writing craft and developing these published stories.

I'm confident that you'll find these stories to be 150 pages of valuable entertainment, and time well spent.

Decades ago the short story held a different place in our culture. In the past 60 years their entertainment value has been replaced by television and iPods, and their literary value has been usurped by a handful of academic journals and pay-to-play, for-profit contests.

Don't get me wrong, I love TV and MP3s as much as the next guy, and certainly have no issue with literary magazines, but these steps have left a certain population of our artists' culture without a home.

In days past, the short story was a stepping stone for aspiring writers. Great authors like John Steinbeck, Ernest Hemingway, Kurt Vonnegut and Stephen King sold short stories to a variety of magazines and publications to jumpstart their careers.

At Columbus Creative Cooperative, it is our goal to recapture this market for local writers. It is our ambition to organize writers into meagerly profitable enterprises, to help steamroll them into their more ambitious pursuits.

So this book is not just a book, it's also a vote. The poll is this: is there still a place in our society for the popular short story? Is this still an art that you appreciate?

If your answer is "yes", then I need you to cast your vote by taking this book and a ten dollar bill up to the nearest person who is standing behind a cash register. If your answer is "absolutely yes" then I need you to buy a copy for a friend as well and email the link to buy this book at ColumbusCoop.org to all of your literate acquaintances.

Only with your support of this project can we provide another anthology in the future, help more aspiring artists, and continue to provide an invaluable outlet for local expression.

If I were any more or less of a hack I would simply reprint Kurt Vonnegut's introduction to *Bagombo Snuff Box* here in its entirety. But being exactly the amount of hack that I am, I'll simply quote my favorite line.

"One monthly that had bought several of my stories [in the 1950s], *Cosmopolitan*, now serves as a harrowingly explicit sex manual." (1999)

In the 1950s, advertisers (and short stories) were moving to television. So magazines began producing less expensive, easier content – self-help.

Printing books is expensive, and in an effort to not pass so much of that cost on to you, dear reader, you'll find in the following pages that we've also brought the advertiser back to the short story. We've made every effort to do so gracefully, and narrowly avoided the temptation to plaster our work with ads like a NASCAR racing machine.

Please support the businesses that support local written

art through Columbus Creative Cooperative.

We'd especially like to thank Sunny Meadows Flower Farm, a local, all-natural flower and vegetable grower, without whose support this project would not be possible. Sunny Meadows provides reasonably priced, all-natural wedding flowers for Central Ohio brides, and also offers subscription pricing for weekly installments of all-natural, seasonal vegetables and chemical-free cut flowers – you can find more information on their website, OurSunnyMeadows.com.

Most of all, thank you, dear reader, for your support of Columbus Creative Cooperative and our first anthology project, *Origins*. Without your strong vote of "yes" to the written word in our local community, this would also be our last anthology project.

It is my ultimate desire that you forever imagine me having written this with a strong drink raised in my hand, instead of sitting on the commode, so let me end with a toast.

"To not checking your messages on the toilet, and long live the local written word."

Plop.

-Brad Pauquette
Director, Columbus Creative Cooperative

For more information about Columbus Creative Cooperative, please visit **ColumbusCoop.org**.

Ben Orlando

Ben Orlando and his wife, Brittany, live in Bexley, just outside of Columbus, with two cats and one frog. There once was a second frog, which may have escaped, or may have been eaten by the remaining frog.

Ben teaches at the Columbus College of Art and Design, and is currently working on a letter-writing project to combat the ever-increasing trend away from print.

The story, "Conditions," deals with the consequences of spite and not seeing what's right in front of our eyes. Ben's second piece, "He Only Wanted a Dollar," is a tragic comedy influenced by Ben's Peace Corps experience in El Salvador.

CONDITIONS
By Ben Orlando

"Have you been waiting here long?" the old man asks me.

I look up from the bench long enough to see his toothy smile, his hopeful eyes. You only see eyes like that, I think, on a lunatic.

"Not long," I tell him and return my eyes to the ground. He takes a seat on the twelve inches of cold metal to my right, when to my left there is more than five feet of space. I slide over to give him more room, and he slides with me. I try to focus on the ground, but I can feel the heat of his stare, so I turn.

My bench mate has a trimmed white beard below a smooth pug nose, and short white hair under a red woolen cap. My senses tell me the man is old, but his pudgy, porcelain face is free of wrinkles. His teeth, also, seem unusually white, and his eyes have no trace of the crows' feet that hound men in their sixties. Or seventies? The longer I stare, the more his appearance confuses me.

And while I stare, he stares back with the same toothy smile, same bulging blue eyes. I can't win this contest and quickly look back at the ground.

"I apologize for my proximity," he tells me. "It's a condition, you see."

"Condition?"

"You should be honored, in fact."

"Is that so?"

"It is," he tells me, and gently takes hold of my coat sleeve. In his dark woolen jacket, tan slacks and thin black loafers, the old man—he must be old—seems underdressed for this bitter February morning. Maybe he's layered.

5

"You ever hear of Haptephobia? Of course you haven't," he says before I can reply. "It's the fear of being touched. You ever hear of the fear of being touched?"

"I guess," I tell him, not getting the point as his fingers sink into my parka sleeve.

"I suffer the opposite," he says, and moves even closer, if that's possible. "Sepraphobia. A fear of not being touched. You don't mind, do you?" His long ear-to-ear grin creates the only lines on his face. "I assure you," he says, "I don't smell."

After sucking in the cold air like the Big Bad Wolf, the old man blows his breath up my nostrils. He could be insane. He could be a monster. But his breath is refreshing and cool. It seems right to believe fresh breath is enough of a reference.

"What happens," I ask the old man, "if you aren't in contact?"

"Oh, I can manage," he says, and pulls back my coat sleeve and the sleeve of my sweater so that his fingers are now wrapped around my wrist. Maybe I should be alarmed, but I'm not.

"Ten minutes, maybe fifteen," he adds, "but after that…"

"What?"

"You might think I'm a bit loony," he tells me, "but there's a phobia for just about everything. For instance, Taphephobia."

"That's…"

"Fear of being buried alive."

"Kind of makes sense."

"It does, it does," he agrees. "But what about Oenophobia, fear of wine, or Lutraphobia, fear of otters?"

"Otters?"

"I told you," he says, "it's insane, this world. People have no idea what they really should be afraid of."

6

These last words come out of his mouth flat and heavy, but the old man quickly recovers and snorts.

"Take chins, for instance."

I try to look at my own while I ask him, "What about them?"

"People are afraid of them, that's what. Geniophobia. And knees," he adds, "and wrists, and fingers, and even that space between your anus and your private merchandise, but I can't recall the name offhand. Compared to those phobias, mine is quite understandable, don't you think?

"Regardless," he continues when I don't respond, "there are a few perks to this condition."

I feel the cold, artificial breeze pushed forward by the advancing city bus as it churns through the slushy black snow of the empty suburb, and passes right on by without even slowing.

"That's the third one," I say, mostly to myself.

"Don't worry," the old man assures me. "Ours will be along soon. Now, do you want to hear about the perks?"

If he were not here, I would sit, and brood. So...

"Why not?" I say, and indulge him.

"I can read people," he tells me. He leans forward, cranes his neck and turns his head to study my eyes full on. I feel as if I'm being probed by an alien.

Just as suddenly, the old man leans back against the bench.

"My word," he mumbles.

"What?"

"That's quite a story. Really. Really."

"Everyone's got a story," I tell him and think, *he can't possibly know*.

"Let's see," he continues. He leans back and lifts his left leg, then his right; settles them around *my* right leg to form a

7

kind of scissor-hold. I could easily overpower him or even tell him to stop, but I don't. He has a condition, after all, and minty fresh breath.

I look around, unable to believe what's happening. But the street in this residential neighborhood is dead. I'm not even quite sure why they have a bus stop in a place where most people have cars. For the teens, I suppose, to find their way into St. Paul.

"Now," he continues, "let's see." He scratches his beard and rubs his pink, puffed-out lips. "You are a man."

"Brilliant. Amazing, really," I say and wonder how long I'll sit here listening to this crap. Forever, I suppose.

"A man in his late twenties," he says, "married, or, was married? Hmmm. You work in...sales."

"Who doesn't?"

"You don't like the cold."

"Who does?"

"In fact you have a condition, a weakness to the cold?"

"No," I tell him. "I don't have any weakness."

"Hypothyroidism?"

"What?"

"Right. Well."

"Well what?"

"Strange," he says. "Something strange has happened. Am I correct?"

I don't answer.

"You are, let me guess, Lebanese."

"Jordanian," I tell him. Big deal.

"Muslim?"

"Not really."

"I'm Frank," he says and tightens his grip on my wrist. "A belated introduction, I suppose. But I'm a good listener," he adds, "and you seem to have a corker on your hands."

"Corker?"

"A burden, a bundle of knots, problems. A Moby Dick of a story. So out with it!"

"Excuse me?"

Somehow, his legs still wrapped around mine, the old man leans forward, cantilevered over the edge, and looks at me with the eyes of an all-knowing father. For all his odd behavior and mannerisms, I can barely resist the urge to confess. Or maybe it is these mannerisms that have created an air of good faith. Still, he is a stranger, and I have to be careful.

Another bus zooms by. I feel like the drivers are intentionally spraying me with blasts of cold air, pouring salt into the wound of their not stopping. Frank waves the bus off like it's a mosquito.

"It's just not the right one," he says. "Now go on, go on."

He reaches into his coat and pulls out a bag of Werther's Originals, and I can't help laughing at such a stereotypical, old-man move. But the act melts what's left of my resolve. I insert the butter candy in my mouth and decide, why the hell not?

"Yesterday," I say, "a middle-aged man knocked on the door, dressed in a ratty blue suit. It was as cold as it is today, but he wasn't wearing a hat. His hair was short, and white. Kind of like...yours."

"Mine?" Frank attempts to look at his hair. "Very well," he says, "now continue."

"The detective," I say, "all he was wearing was that suit. No gloves. My wife, Sharon, was still in her pajamas. She hadn't left the house in a week and was reluctant to see anyone. But she opened the door and stared for a while at this guy in the doorway, until he reached into his pocket and held up his badge.

"'Are you Mrs. Libdeh?' he asked her."

Frank pops a Werther's into his mouth. "Some people," he says, "don't mind the cold."

"Now, Sharon," I say, ignoring Frank's comment, "with her usual charm, was about to slam the door in this guy's face when he says, as if he doesn't much care one way or the other, 'I have information about Robert Abdella.'"

"This man," Frank asks me, "he is a police man, yes?"

"A detective."

"But what—"

I lift my left hand to wave him quiet because Frank is now holding onto my right hand. "So Sharon," I continue, "just stood there for a good twenty seconds until finally she said, 'What about him?'

"'I have information,' the detective tells her, 'about how he died.'"

"Hold on!" Frank shouts. "Who is Robert Abdella?"

"My full name," I tell Frank, "is Robert Abdella Libdeh."

"You? But clearly—"

"Do you want to hear this or not?"

Frank nods, and again leans back.

"So Sharon, her voice rising, tells the detective, 'I know how he died. The son of a bitch drowned. Now get the hell out!'"

"Wait!" Frank lifts his hand for me to stop, and again I look around to see if anyone is present to notice the old, wrinkle-less, well-groomed Santa Claus snuggling up to a twenty-eight-year-old Arab American. But still, the neighborhood is silent.

"Please," Frank insists. "It would help to provide some background."

"For instance?"

"For instance?" Frank shakes his head as if I'm the lunatic. "Where were you during this conversation?"

"I was at the top of the stairs."

"But your wife just said—"

"The week before…" I look down, pause, consider closing my mouth and ignoring him until the next bus arrives. Or maybe walk away. No. I won't do that. The door is open and I don't want to stop. I decide to tell Frank what I've told no one.

"I drowned in the lake."

"Excuse me?" Frank seems flustered, but the news of my death does not slacken his grip. He remains pressed against me as if we were bound by an invisible rope.

"At least," I add, "that's what I wanted the world to think. Last Tuesday I rowed out into the middle of Lake Noawak with all my supplies, and then I just … disappeared."

"So they thought—"

"That I'd drowned."

"But in fact—"

"I'd been living in our bedroom closet."

Frank seems pleased and troubled at the same time.

"To the world," I say, "it was an accident. But not to Sharon. I left her a special note blaming her and only her for my death."

Frank shakes his head. "That doesn't sound very nice."

"Yeah, well, Sharon isn't very nice. In fact, she's a fucking reptile."

"But you married her."

"Guilt's a powerful thing. I owed my parents for my childhood."

"A bit dramatic, don't you think, Robert?"

"Two demolished cars," I tell him, "three major scandals, eight school transfers, my little sister, the exchange student, the—"

"Your little sister?"

"I avoided the wedding for years. I made excuses, traveled, but the fear of not knowing when it would happen finally got to me. I agreed to the marriage even though both Sharon and I were who we were from the start. My side had the prestige, and her family had money. A perfect old-world union."

"Hmmph." Frank crunches his candy and squeezes his eyes shut, deep in thought. "Could she really have been that bad?"

"Once," I say, "a waitress forgot to use non-dairy creamer in Sharon's coffee. Sharon casually tossed the scalding liquid onto the girl's skirt. Another time, for my birthday, she gave me one of those sonar fisherman devices. I almost never went fishing, but after a week, when I hadn't taken the thing out of the box, she called me out to the driveway so I could watch her run the thing over with her Lexus. She was crying, but not for me."

"That doesn't make sense—" Frank begins, but I cut him off.

"Once during a funeral, while the father of my dead cousin was giving the eulogy, Sharon answered a cell call from one of her clients. She didn't hang up or lower her voice, just held a normal conservation while everyone stared. No one could talk. They were stunned. They couldn't believe a human being was capable of such apathy. That's Sharon."

Frank stares at the ground. I can see his mind working, trying to come to Sharon's defense. "Surely," he says, but he can't think of a response.

"She doesn't like to kill things," I tell him, knowing this is her only redeeming quality.

Again Frank seems flustered.

"The reason she doesn't like to kill things," I explain, "is because she doesn't like the guilt that comes with killing something, as if simply wounding or severely burning is perfectly fine. For some reason, even Sharon's twisted mind can't brush off murder.

"Once, she accidentally ran over a squirrel and tried to deny it, but I convinced her that the little guy was perfectly healthy before she crushed it under the tires. For the next week the ghost of that squirrel followed her everywhere. I swear to God, I'd walk into the kitchen and find her arguing with it. 'It was an accident you little rat!' she'd scream and try to hit it with a spatula."

"I suppose," Frank says, and again comes up empty, "that's…something."

"But even this flaw couldn't last. Sharon's a fighter, and no matter how much it scared her, she eventually decided she had to defeat her demons. Not just defeat them, but crush them."

"Admirable," Frank mutters, and inserts another piece of candy into his mouth. In his awkward position, leaned back against the bench and straddling my leg, he seems like a child climbing around on Santa's lap. And given *his* appearance, the image in my head is tending toward Escher or Picasso.

"So she was seeking a therapeutic solution?" Frank suggests. "What's wrong with—"

"Her idea of therapy was to start killing as many little animals as fast as she could."

"No."

"Yes. Around the house she trampled ants and worms. She started leaving cookies out to attract the mice. On the road she swerved into squirrels and birds, and by the lake she aimed for the ducks."

"Ducks?"

"Quack-quack, you know?"

"I know what a duck is."

"'It's therapy,' she'd tell me and anyone who discovered her little pastime. In her mind her actions were perfectly justified."

Frank looks down and scratches his beard. "But you say she had problems after killing just one squirrel."

"Oh, she had major problems with her new methods," I tell him. "She'd lock herself in the bedroom and fight with the ghosts for days. But as time went by, she fought less, seemed more at ease. But Sharon was not satisfied. She needed to beat it once and for all."

"I'm afraid to ask."

"She bought a shotgun."

"A shotgun?"

"During the weekends she'd drive out to the woods and kill chipmunks by the handful, sparrows by the dozen. She'd brag about dropping a rabbit or groundhog, and somehow, the more animals she killed, the better she became at dealing with the after effect. And that took away my last bit of control."

"What *do* you mean, Robert?" Frank tightens his grip on my wrist.

"I mean, every once in a while—not often, but say, two, three times a year—I'd… arrange things so Sharon would find herself the murderer of a small woodland creature, or a cockroach or ant, even. That squirrel I told her she'd crushed? It was already dead. When she did something, when she went too far, I used her guilt and her fears as a sort of punishment, a balance. I figured, while she was haunted by little animals, she wouldn't hurt bigger things, like people."

"Hmm." Frank pulls his cap tight around his ears. "Is that why you tricked her?"

I don't like his tone and simply glare in response.

"So Sharon didn't know you were playing with her?"

"Not on the surface, but I think some part of her knew. I think. I'm sure."

Frank leans back, stretches and yawns, and then I yawn. Again I stare out at the cookie-cutter suburbs, at the snow on the lawns and the leftover gaudy ornaments from Christmas. Soon there will be giant inflated bunnies and pastel eggs hung from the rooftops.

"I don't understand," Frank says and wraps his left arm around my back. It seems if he could, he'd attach himself at the hip. "What does this have to do with the detective, and you contriving your death?"

"The detective," I tell him, "ruined everything. Like I said, Sharon was starting to get the best of her demons, and at the same time I'd had it. I tried to please my family, stayed married for four years. Sharon and I had our own everything—beds, cars, closets, refrigerators. We hardly talked to each other, but still it was unbearable. And yet divorce wasn't an option."

"Your family?"

"My father. So I thought of another way out, while at the same time I figured I could get in one last jab. I settled on the ultimate guilt trip."

"So you went out to the lake…"

"I made sure to talk to a dozen people on the way. I also set up a meeting that day so somebody would be looking for me. I parked the car near the first dock."

"You had a boat?"

"I'd been borrowing it from our neighbor, and I asked him that morning if I could take it out. Just a simple aluminum shell with two oars. I started going out a month earlier to build a routine. On the weekends there were a few guys here and there, but on a Tuesday I knew it'd be empty. So I packed my wetsuit

15

and a change of clothes in a sealable plastic bag."

"So you rowed out, and then left the boat? You swam?"

"Sure."

"Why didn't you just push the boat into the water?"

I smile, trying not to feel too smug. "A ranger," I tell Frank, "came around every day at 10 a.m. and 3 p.m. to smoke a joint. He only stopped by for a few minutes each time, but he was the perfect witness to say he saw me out there in the middle of the lake.

"The second he finished making his first loop that morning, I slipped into the wetsuit, grabbed my bag and jumped in."

Frank looks at me now with a sad smile. "There was a tear in your wetsuit."

"How'd you—? Right, your condition," I say. I don't know how Frank could know about the suit, but that's not for now.

"It was cold," I tell him, "and I really hadn't expected it to be such a pain in the ass. A few times I thought...anyway, eventually the pain faded, my body went numb and I pushed on until I was at the dock pulling myself up. There was an inch of snow on the ground, so I carried a pine tree branch behind me and did my best to erase my trail. It was an eight-mile hike back to the house, and I knew Sharon would be at work when I snuck in."

"So nobody figured it out?"

"C'mon, Frank. People only see what's right in front of them. I didn't have any close friends who would think me capable of such a thing, and my parents certainly wouldn't fathom it. I mean, if a guy doesn't tell you he's going to do it, would you ever suspect?"

"Did you think about what you were going to do," Frank asks me, "after you had your fun with your wife?" He speaks

16

these last words with clear disapproval. I don't think it's possible to convince him my actions weren't petty. I still believe they were justified.

"I purchased a cabin in Arizona with cash. I figured I could hang for a while in the heat and figure things out." I don't tell Frank I'd sold Sharon's inherited earrings to pay for the cabin, or that I'd been planning on stealing her car as the final 'screw you' until the detective in the blue suit arrived and made public transit the better option.

Frank shakes his head and smiles. "So you'd been living in your closet."

I'm happy to see him, for the moment, not condemning me.

"Was there a funeral?"

"They're still searching for the body," I tell him.

"And Sharon had no idea? You walking around in the same house for a week?"

"Like I said, it doesn't matter if it's right under your nose. If you have a certain perception, that's the way it is. Sharon had no clue, and when she did hear something, she thought it was my ghost haunting her. A few times she screamed, 'Robert! Leave me alone. It wasn't my fault!' and went running from the room."

I laugh, but Frank doesn't seem to find the memory amusing.

We sit for a while in silence. I wonder if he's trying to make a final judgment, or if he's just thinking.

"And yesterday, the detective?" he says.

"I didn't hear his name, but he told Sharon he worked for the St. Paul Police Department, and he was investigating my death." Frank's expression is similar, I think, to my reaction when I heard the detective deliver this news.

"He asked to come in," I tell Frank, "even though he was already standing in the foyer.

"'What the hell is this about?' Sharon said, clearly wanting it out and done with.

"'Your husband,' the man said, 'was seen at the lake with a woman who fits your description.'

"'What?' Sharon laughed in his face. 'I was with a client all day. This is…you're insane! Get out of here!'

"'Yesterday a witness came forward,' the detective told her, not reacting in the least to her command. 'And since then,' he continued, 'we've been making some phone calls. My partner is in the car. I didn't think he would be necessary.'

"'Necessary?' Sharon looked down and considered the word. She didn't understand. Neither did I.

"'Call my work!' she screamed. 'They'll tell you. Call Albert Hemmings. He'll tell you!'

"'We called both,' the detective said, and grabbed Sharon's wrist. 'They both said they hadn't seen you all day, said you called in sick. Now if you would come with me, Mrs. Libdeh.'"

I pause to visualize what happened next, to take a breath, but Frank is impatient.

"Did she go," he asks. "Did she resist? The shotgun. Did she grab the shotgun?"

"No. The detective grabbed her, dragged her out of the house. I watched from the upstairs window while they tucked her into the back of the cruiser."

"But she was in her pajamas? Isn't that what you said?"

"That's how it happened," I say. "She was screaming it was a suicide, screaming about the letter I wrote, but they didn't stop, didn't listen."

"And now?"

"And now she's at the station." I feel a grin tug at the corner of my mouth. "The prime suspect in this charade."

Frank glares at me. "Robert, did you have anything—"

"Of course not! I wouldn't do that. I have no idea why they said those things. There was nobody at the lake but me, and the patrol when he came through. And I know Sharon went to work. It doesn't make any sense."

I look to Frank for an answer, but Frank's eyes and mind are elsewhere. Since he's not looking, I stare even longer—at his smooth white face, his red woolen hat.

"He was wearing a hat," I say mostly to myself. I remember watching them take Sharon away. When the car began to pull out from the curb, I started to turn away from the window. I can see it now, the detective, in the passenger seat, slipping something onto his head. "A red hat."

"What?" Frank returns to our world.

"The detective." I pause. "In the car, he pulled on a red woolen cap. Just like yours."

"Robert. You're making no sense."

"And he wasn't wearing a coat."

"It's not a secret," Frank tells me. "If you keep the extremities warm, you barely need to cover your middle regions. Now, your wife."

"I could swear it was the same."

Frank shakes his head. "Think about your wife. All you have to do is show them you're not dead, and they cannot hold her. She'll go free."

"Maybe."

"No, Robert. No maybe."

"I told you, Frank, I don't know what the hell's going on! I can't just walk in and say 'Surprise! I faked my death. It's all a big misunderstanding.'"

"Why not?"

"You don't just—"

"You fear the repercussions."

"That's not it! I just...I don't know. I should wait."

"Robert," he says. "You are not waiting. You are running. There is no struggle. There is no question. Unless."

"Unless what?"

Frank lowers his head and begins to move away from me. He releases his grip, and I feel like I've been ripped in half.

"Frank, what is it?" An hour ago I didn't know this man, thought he was a lunatic or at least senile, but now I don't want him to leave. I need his opinions, and most of all I need his approval. But Frank merely shakes his head and pulls his red woolen cap down over his ears.

"You want this to fall on her."

"That's not true!"

"Of course it is, Robert! You want her to suffer. You've said as much."

"But not this," I tell him. "This is too much."

"Well," he says, "there's no more to say."

For a while we don't speak. Ten minutes pass. The day is cold and still. When I move my face, I feel it crack. In the distance, I hear the humming of the bus, the churning of gears as it accelerates, pauses, accelerates.

Frank crunches another Werther's.

I know I could walk back to the house, make a phone call, or walk to the police station two miles east. I try to picture Sharon suffering, trembling, sobbing as the coatless detective threatens her life, her safety, her future and somehow ties her to this ludicrous murder. I try to feel sympathy for Sharon and search my mind for the good times, try to feel something other than hate, spite, revenge; but the rage only grows, expands in my head like foam. I cannot forgive her, I cannot let her off the hook, whatever this is, whatever happens. She deserves it. She deserves it.

Frank is a few inches—may as well be a mile—from me now, staring at the ground, hands folded in his lap, muttering as the bus approaches. From the wind, from the sounds, I know this time it will stop.

I stand up. I have a small duffel with me, some cash. Frank doesn't move.

"You're not coming?" I ask him. Frank looks as if he might cry. It's the separation, I think. His phobia. He's suffering from withdrawal.

"One for the road?" he says, and digs another butter candy from his pocket. I feel like I'm in a commercial. Or at least, like someone's watching me.

I take the Werther's and walk to the bus, climb the stairs and hand the driver a dollar without looking. I'm looking at Frank.

After I hand the driver my dollar, I feel strange, dizzy, but I am not spinning. My life is spinning around me, almost as if it has been compressed into a toilet and someone pulled the cord, and I'm looking down, watching it go.

The bus starts to move, but I continue to stand next to the driver. I stare out through the windshield at a world that is dull, skewed, tainted. I know something is happening, but I'm not sure what until the doors close, sealing me in, and the truth hits me like I've just woken from a dream and seen everything with perfect, horrifying clarity.

When I begin to walk towards the back, and I see Frank sitting to my right, I am not surprised.

"Right under my nose," I say.

Frank nods sadly. I think of the wetsuit, the leak, the

frigid cold in my bones as I swam through the icy lake. I had not practiced. I had read reports, assumed I would be okay, and as I swam, minute by minute, the desperation I felt, the paralyzing cold, were eventually replaced by no feeling at all. I went under a few times but came up determined to finish, and I continued to swim, looking forward, only forward, as if part of me knew, if I had looked back, I would have seen myself.

I climbed onto the dock, feeling strange but satisfied, and walked through the woods, careful to erase the footprints behind me as I quickly erased the truth from my mind.

Standing next to Frank, I think of Sharon, and the detective in the blue suit. No coat, like Frank. Same hair, like Frank. Same hat, like Frank.

"If I had said I'd come forward," I say, "explained to the police I wasn't dead…"

Frank doesn't speak, so I keep talking.

"It had nothing to do with Sharon. The detective, he was like…you. And the whole murder thing? That wasn't real? That was for me?"

How, I don't know. Did they really take Sharon away? Did she ever leave the house? I haven't a clue how these worlds intersect, overlap. I just got here, after all.

"Frank," I say, and begin to tremble. My legs give out and I sink to the floor. I look around. There are no other passengers.

"Frank. Where am I going?"

Frank gives me his quiet grandfatherly smile, and pats the seat next to him. I crawl across him and climb onto the green vinyl near the window. I take his hand. I've never wanted so badly to touch another person.

"Here, in this place," he says, and nods toward the gray scenery through the window, "it is a condition. But where we are going, when there is a chance, you will take comfort in this." Frank wraps his hands around mine and squeezes, and the warmth in his fingers and palms radiates through my skin, spreads throughout my body. Suddenly I am chilled to the bone, and Frank is the fire.

"Frank? Where are we going?"

I can barely hold it together. I remember lying in bed as a child, in an empty house, in the dark, the creaking and groaning from a thousand unknown places, the hysterical fear of not knowing from where the monsters would come. The blindness. This is similar, but much worse.

"Frank?"

Frank looks towards the front of the bus, where I now realize there is no longer a driver. Is Frank the next to go? Will I be alone? Will the bus disappear? And leave me…

The thought is paralyzing.

"Frank? For Christ's sake, where are we going?"

Frank gives me a look—sad, resigned—that warrants no reply. *Please*, he says without speaking. *Don't ask me to answer.*

He doesn't look at me again. But he doesn't disappear, and continues to hold my hand.

Funny. Right now, I have the overwhelming urge to kill myself.

HE ONLY WANTED A DOLLAR

By Ben Orlando

It was Polavoe's suggestion to turn the crackhead into a maid, and as usual, everyone thought he was crazy.

They were sitting on the patio of ex-Peace Corps volunteer Jasper Rutgen's apartment ten minutes north of La Estancia in a peaceful, upscale San Salvador neighborhood, surrounded by ten-foot metal gates and brick walls covered in razor wire and broken glass. It was Saturday morning.

Jasper shared the four-bedroom apartment with three other ex-volunteers who'd decided to remain in the gang-infested, earthquake-prone country after their two years and three months of service had ended. Even with gangs and violence and dirty water and toilets that didn't accept toilet paper, they wanted to stay. Even with constant diarrhea, sultry days, five months of drought and hopelessness around every corner, to these Americans, life was still better there than it was in the States.

Angie Brian, twenty-nine with supple limbs, enormous, back-aching breasts, long red hair and a sweet, freckled face, landed a job five months earlier running a Catholic housing charity, mostly telling people how to tell other people how to build mud houses. She did her best to ignore the constant cult-like proselytizing that went into every poorly-constructed charity home, and promised herself, as always, that she'd return home soon.

Angie sipped her Bloody Mary and asked Polavoe, "Are you insane?" as if she were angry, when in fact she loved Polavoe for creating the nonsense that allowed her to not think about more serious things.

"You must be insane," Angie said through a smile, as the Crackhead poked his dirty head through the steel bars that separated the patio from the sidewalk. He asked again for a dollar.

Polavoe, mostly because he was not one of the four apartment dwellers, suggested again that they make the Crackhead work for his money. He knew that Anderson, a new roommate and fugitive ever since he was kicked out of Peace Corps, would see Polavoe's idea as the perfect move in the game of self-aggrandizement.

"He is, most assuredly, insane," said Jasper, who wiped the pitch-black curls from his sun-weathered face. He shoved another forkful of cheddar omelet past his sunburned lips and said, "That doesn't mean he's always wrong."

Jasper swallowed and burped. "But in this case, Polavoe," he continued, "you're both."

"Maybe," Anderson said, shoveling his gourmet creation past his meaty red lips, "our friend Polavoe's onto something here, if you think about the roots of shame."

"Not again," said Jasper.

"He's a crack head," Angie complained and searched the bottom of her glass for more Bloody Mary.

"But the crack is just a fill. We're all abused when we're young," Anderson told them. "But some of us,"—he turned his gaze on Jasper—"are more abused than others. Deep scars; deep, deep scars come from name calling, from comparing you to someone else. Jasper, who were you compared to?"

"No one," Jasper barked. "I was an only child, you dick."

"Anyway," Anderson continued, "the Crackhead here

probably faced obstacles we couldn't even imagine. If you give a guy a chance—"

"He'll steal your Jeep," Angie told Anderson, and walked off to find more vodka and tomatoes. Anderson bought the Jeep she referred to with money he made selling marijuana to Peace Corps volunteers through a grower in Guatemala.

Anderson loved his Jeep; his Jeep didn't love him. It refused to start since the day he drove it to the triple-X video store. Fifteen hundred dollars and six weeks later, the 1974 pea-green model was growing mold.

"Anyway" Anderson said, watching Angie's ass as she departed, "You give a man options, and you give him a chance. You give a man a chance, and you give him... possibilities!"

All the while, the Crackhead, his face pressed against the cool steel bars, patiently waited while the fat American blathered on in a language he couldn't and didn't want to understand. He just wanted one dollar for Christ's sake to run around the corner and buy a tiny packet of crack to tide him over for the rest of the day. But what happened next blew the Crackhead's already-drug-blown mind.

"Quieres un trabapo?" Anderson asked, staring directly at the Crackhead with a benevolent, royal smile, lifting his blue t-shirt and rubbing his fat hairy belly to give the proposal authenticity.

"It's 'trabajo'," Polavoe corrected.

"Shut up," Anderson hissed, and stared expectantly at the dirty young man before him.

A job? What the hell is this guy talking about? thought the Crackhead, who hadn't worked since he was a little boy running errands for his drug-dealing older brother, now chopped up and spread out across the Pan-American Highway.

The Crackhead knew that working—really working—got a man killed. He knew he was better off begging. Begging brought no loyalties, no burdens, no obligations. Somebody threatens you, tries to reel you into their back-stabbing schemes, you just walk away, start begging somewhere else.

Yes sir, begging is the life of the free man, thought the Crackhead. *I may be dirty. I may be hungry, and thirsty, and horny, and sleepy, and sore, and all around miserable, but nobody's going to make me do any work, drag me down into a life of fear and servitude. Hell no. Not me.*

The Crackhead looked down for a while at his feet, hard to distinguish from a pile of dirt. He looked at his pants, more like scraps of torn denim slapped onto weedy legs poking through the tears, the skin sucked tight to the bones. And then he looked up.

"Que trabajo," he said, because it didn't hurt to inquire.

"Limpiando," said the fat American who reminded the Crackhead of Sylvester Stallone. The Crackhead thought Chris Farley was Sylvester Stallone.

"Limpiando y organizando las cosas en la casa," Anderson continued.

Cleaning and arranging? Was he crazy? The Crackhead had no interest in cleaning, and if he was cleaning, did that mean he had to be clean? How could he clean if he was dirty? Would they hose him down like they did in the prison? Would they give him a uniform? A uniform meant a set of clothes that completely covered his body, which might be a good thing, but then he'd have to keep the uniform clean, and he had no interest in doing that.

"Cuanto," he asked the fat man.

"C'mon, Anderson," Jasper squealed. "Enough already.

This is my—"

"Shhh," Anderson hissed. "Let me finish, will you?" He turned back to the Crackhead.

"Tres horas cada selama."

"It's 'semana'."

"Shut up."

"Cuanto," the Crackhead repeated.

Anderson rolled his fat tongue across his big lips. "Mmmm, veinte dolares."

"Twenty dollars!" Angie screamed from the kitchen. "Are you crazy? Eight dollars is the average daily income. Daily!"

"Oh c'mon," Anderson said. "That's five dollars from each of us."

"Luger's not even here," Jasper complained—knowing Luger, the fourth and most sloth-like roommate, would have no problem with this arrangement.

Anderson ignored the rebuttal. He turned back to the Crackhead while Polavoe subtly smiled, sat back, sipped his delicious cup of fresh Salvadoran coffee imported from San Francisco, and quietly delighted in the mess he'd play no part in, after this.

Yet the Crackhead did not respond. He was flummoxed. *Twenty dollars? For three hours cleaning this jerk's house? That was a lot of money. But what about my freedom?* he thought. *He might try to get me to do other work, to make promises and then I might end up spread out across the Pan American like my stupid ass brother.*

The Crackhead looked up and told the fat American, "Okay, Bob," and hated himself for agreeing.

"Me llamo Anderson," said Anderson.

"Okay, Bob," the Crackhead repeated.

He pretended to listen to the fat American explain how he had to show up every Saturday at noon and work until 3 p.m.; how he had to take a bath or at least make himself presentable because there was no use cleaning when you're downright filthy; how he had to meet and greet each one of the housemates beginning the following week in order to create an atmosphere of calm and understanding and cultural brotherhood.

Angie walked out onto the patio with her fresh bloody drink as Anderson reached his hand through the bars to seal the deal. She shrugged.

"He's going to steal your Jeep," she said, "and no way in hell's he coming into my room."

"Ditto," said Jasper.

"No te precupes," Anderson told the Crackhead, who was already starting to panic.

For a moment, Polavoe felt guilty for instigating this arrangement. He wasn't supposed to interfere, according to the life philosophy he'd adopted three weeks earlier. But maybe, he thought, it will work out.

"Hasta la selama proxima," Anderson told the Crackhead and retracted his now-filthy hand.

"Por favor," said the Crackhead, seeing no benefit to this meeting if he didn't come away with money, right now. "Necesito dinero. Algo, ahora."

"Patience," said the fat American, and flapped his pasty arms across his Seattle Mariner's t-shirt.

"Por favor," pleaded the Crackhead, who saw no value in patience or hard work or any work. "Un dolar."

"Give him the goddamn dollar," said Jasper, no longer able to stand the toilet-like odor emanating from the Crackhead's personal space.

"I don't have anything…," Anderson admitted. He dug into his pockets and came up empty.

The Crackhead began to panic. So much promise, and now…

Out of frustration he reached into his pocket, wrapped his fingers around the sharp five-inch piece of metal he carried around just in case.

"Wait," said Polavoe, and unknowingly saved Anderson from a stabbing.

He pulled three quarters, three dimes and two nickels from his pocket and dropped the coins into the Crackhead's hands without touching them. *After all*, Polavoe thought, *I just created something special. An opportunity on all fronts, and that's surely worth a hundred and fifteen cents.*

"Hasta luego!" Anderson said, and reveled in his generosity and foresight while the Crackhead walked away.

I can't wait for some crack, the Crackhead thought. *And I can't wait to steal that fucker's Jeep.*

The next week, the Crackhead arrived an hour late and asked for his twenty dollars.

"Primero, trabajo," Anderson said. He opened the front gate and led the Crackhead into the apartment, where Jasper and Angie immediately covered their noses.

"He bloody reeks," Angie said.

"Tell him if he wants his money," Jasper shouted, "he has to take a goddamn bath or something!"

So Anderson reluctantly told the Crackhead to come back the next week freshly bathed.

"Mi dinero?" the Crackhead asked.

"No dinero," Anderson said and led the dirty young man to the gate, wanting to instill in the Crackhead some work ethic. "La proxima selama."

"It's 'semana'!"

"Screw off!" Anderson told Angie and led the Crackhead outside.

Confused and angry, the Crackhead found himself standing in the middle of the street without any money before he fully realized what had happened, and cursed himself for not stabbing the fat American when he had the chance.

The next week, he returned on time after stopping off at the nearby café to clean up in the men's room sink. This time his reek was tolerable, but his cleaning method was not, for he had none. His method was to fill a bucket with water, dump the water on the floor and swirl it around for a while with his blackened feet.

"You need to teach him how to clean because he clearly doesn't know what the hell he's doing!" Angie screamed from her bedroom before closing and locking her door.

For the next hour Anderson showed the Crackhead how to organize objects, how to clean the floors, how to scrub the toilet and do the dishes. Anderson had never worked so hard in his life.

"Comprende?" he asked the Crackhead at the end of the hour.

"Si," said the Crackhead. "Donde esta mi dinero?"

"No. No haga." Anderson squeezed his nose into his eyes. "No haga. No…Jasper!"

After a long minute, Jasper poked his head out of his room.

"I need a translator," Anderson said.

"Jesus, Anderson. You've been here two years!"

"That's beside the point."

Jasper smiled and slammed his door.

"Asshole!" Anderson grabbed the Crackhead's toothpick arm and led him to the other side of the house.

"Angie!"

Angie's door slowly opened. Her red hair appeared, then her face, filled with a scowl.

"Please," Anderson whined. "Translate."

Angie rolled her eyes but stayed.

"Okay," Anderson began. "You didn't do anything today, so—"

"You can't say that?"

"Just translate!"

"Hoy, no hiciste nada," she told the Crackhead.

"And the only way you'll learn," Anderson continued,"is to work for your money. Come back next week, clean the house, do a good job, and you'll get your twenty dollars."

While Angie translated, Anderson led the Crackhead outside, and before he knew what was happening, the Crackhead once again found himself in the middle of the street with no money in his pocket.

Over the next week, the Crackhead wavered between never returning to the house full of obnoxious Americans, and stalking them until he had an opportunity to beat them and steal from them what he deserved. But when Saturday morning came around, the Crackhead, slightly strung out, found himself knocking on the metal gate once again, smelling of men's room soap—his face shaved, his hair slicked back—ready to work and really get that twenty dollars for Christ's sake.

For the next three hours the Crackhead organized the

kitchen in an orderly and logical manner. He cleaned the toilet and floors and washed the dishes. He arranged the books in the bookshelf according to color and dumped miscellaneous trash in the back of the hallway closet.

"Wow," Angie said, poking her freckled head from her bedroom to see her surroundings cleaner than they'd ever been.

"Holy shit," said Jasper as he stepped out of his room and stared in awe at the Crackhead's handiwork.

Anderson beamed for the Crackhead and for his successful experiment in social engineering. He was proud of the filthy street child, like a man might be proud of a hamster or ferret. He slapped the Crackhead on the back and handed the weary young man four crisp five-dollar bills.

"Buen trabapo," he told the Crackhead. "Don't you feel good after a hard day's work?"

Before the Crackhead could tell Anderson to go screw himself, Anderson added, "Hasta luego," and walked into the kitchen to make a meatball sandwich.

With nothing more to do, the Crackhead tucked his earnings into his underwear and walked outside with the keys he'd stolen from Anderson's pocket.

He tried to start the Jeep, but to his great annoyance, it wouldn't turn over. So he ducked his head under the open hood of the broken-down vehicle and removed the brand new battery Anderson had purchased just the day before. Then he grabbed a rag from the ground and walked out the front gate with the rag-cushioned battery resting atop his head.

When Polavoe passed the Crackhead on the street, he thought nothing of the battery on his head, but he did notice the almost-clean odor emanating from the normally filthy young man.

"Hola," Polavoe said to the Crackhead.

"Eat shit, Gringo," the Crackhead told Polavoe, and bobbled down the street balancing the car battery.

"The Crackhead just told me to eat shit," Polavoe said when Anderson opened the gate.

Anderson shrugged. "Maybe he doesn't like you."

"Maybe he doesn't like you."

Anderson guffawed. He didn't like the idea of people not liking him unless he didn't like them first. "I just gave him twenty dollars," Anderson told Polavoe. "Why would you say that?"

"No reason," Polavoe replied and passed the useless Jeep as he climbed the three concrete steps into the sparkling clean house.

"Wow," Povaloe said and whistled to properly display his appreciation for the tidy, glowing surroundings.

"He did a good job, didn't he?" Anderson said as Jasper and Angie emerged from their rooms to admire the work of the man they still didn't want to employ.

"He sure did," said Povaloe. "So I wonder why he hates you so much."

"Why do you keep saying that?!" Anderson shouted.

"No reason," Polavoe said, and walked into the kitchen for a beer. "Except a few minutes ago I saw the Crackhead walking down the street with your car battery on his head."

"You, you saw what?" Anderson stuttered.

"Yeah," Angie confirmed. "I watched him through my window. He seemed pretty angry."

Anderson tried to laugh as he casually, anxiously walked outside, and then screamed like a man stabbed in the stomach when he saw the empty cavity where his brand new battery should have been.

Anderson ran to the gate, yelling, "Why would he do such a thing?!"

"I guess he did hate you," Angie said, now standing in the doorway next to Polavoe with her hands on her hips.

"Yeah," said Jasper. "A sneaky little bugger, that Crackhead."

"But I was just trying to help him!" Anderson shouted. He opened the gate, and hopelessly speed-waddled down the street in search of his battery and the monster he'd created.

"I guess he didn't want your help!" Polavoe screamed.

"Of course he did!" Anderson replied, his voice fading as he ambled out of range.

Polavoe and Angie drank a six pack of Pilsner tallboys and watched the first half of Alien 3 dubbed in Spanish.

"I'm hungry," Angie said as the Alien devoured a platoon. She and Polavoe left the house, turned left on Alomeda, and then walked right on Avenida Lutera, toward El Café Sunzal.

At the corner, they found Anderson on his knees, holding his stomach, dripping blood from somewhere under his hands.

Kim Younkin

Kim is a Columbus native who's been writing short stories for most of her life—a few of them even worth reading. She believes a good story can soothe just about any ailment.

She swears she had the inspiration for her featured story "Clarity" before the recent release of a major commercial film with a similar dénouement!

Kim is a contributing short story and skit writer at ActivityConnection.com. Her own stories have appeared online and in Adams Media's *A Cup of Comfort* series. She is a former humor columnist for *Columbus Parent* magazine, and she laughs at a lot at her own jokes.

Kim lives in Upper Arlington with her husband and two young sons—who seem to also have a natural love of the writing craft. Kim enjoys watching them create on their own early literary adventures.

CLARITY
By Kim Younkin

"It won't budge," Hack said, his voice low, full of gravel. Under his black ski cap, his blond eyebrows furrowed over his dark gray eyes.

He's worried, Ella thought. *He never worries.*

Hack jerked Ella's bare forearm again, hard, making needle points of blood on her wrist.

She winced but hardly moved. She was crouched in a squat with her right coat sleeve pulled up to her elbow and her hand stuck fast in a rock hole. Infant tendrils of panic swirled inside her under her lightweight, zero-degree climbing garb. But she fought it, and said to Hack with a half-smile, "Kind of like you. Always holding on."

On his knees in the packed snow next to her, Tim Hackman looked squarely into Ella's brown eyes, unsmiling. "Glad you noticed. Now let's think."

Ella's hand was numbing from the cold. It scared her; she'd never been able to endure even a Midwestern winter day without gloves. Yet here she was, her Gore-Tex cold weather climbing glove lying worthless on the ground beside her.

"I already know what you're thinking," she said, looking away.

"Really?" Hack asked, pulling on her arm again. "And what's that?"

"That I'm an idiot. More trouble than I'm worth."

He paused. Ella still didn't look at him.

"I just don't know how this could've happened, Ella. It's not even…logical."

"What?" she asked. "The hole? Or me shoving my hand in it?"

"Both."

She turned back and stared at him. His cold-chapped face was blank, his eyes wary.

"Hack, I saw something in there. I swear to God." Ella yanked her arm in frustration. The needle points of blood on her wrists became drops. "So let's say the blame is mine. That way we can get past the part where you're thinking it and resenting me, and focus on getting me out of here."

She had been an idiot, after all.

They'd broken camp for the day and hiked three hours toward the mountain's summit when they came upon two massive, towering rock walls—colossal Stonehenge-type structures that looked as if God had dropped them straight from the sky. After a few minutes of ogling, Hack had sat down a few feet away, resting, eyes closed and head thrown back, gulping from his water bottle. Ella took off her hot fleece hat and pulled back her long black hair to breathe some crisp air, lazily walking and running her free right hand along the walls. Something had caught her eye, glinting in a slit of frigid sunlight in an odd, holey crevice at the walls' joint. And for no reason, she'd wanted it.

Impulsively, she'd dropped her hair, ripped off her glove and thrust her hand into the hole. And as she stretched her fingers to grope for the object inside, the walls swelled— she swore they did—and closed around her, trapping her. She hesitated in surprise, and in that fraction of a second she couldn't pull herself out. She pulled and yanked and tried to free herself. Then she grew frantic, and stopped.

Now, here they were—three days into this climbing trip, several hundred feet up, alone, with her hand clamped in a four-inch hole.

Ella inhaled raggedly. She turned from Hack's gaze and rested her forehead against the rock. Her knees burned from the stress of squatting; she shifted and sat down on the snow. The cold shot immediately through her snow pants.

Think, she told herself. *Just try to think.*

Hack turned Ella's forearm and pulled on it again, said nothing of blame. He nodded at the hole. "Do you have any idea what's in there?" he asked.

Ella stretched her trapped fingers, reaching. She thought her fingertips brushed up against something—something not rock, not cold and hard—but then it was gone, and she didn't know whether she'd really felt anything at all.

She sighed. "The hole's too deep. I can't touch anything."

Damn, stupid fool, she thought.

The trip had been Hack's idea; Ella had just come along, ambivalent. Like with most things in her life, she hadn't really cared one way or another. She was indecisive to a fault. She didn't know if her indecision caused her general ambivalence or was a result of it—the two thorns had always just grown together.

It's not that she didn't want to feel something certain. Ella had always longed for clarity, even just once. Even just about a climbing trip. A thought of *sure I'll go; I love the mountains* or *God, no, I can't stand the outdoors*—a clear answer with no dangling, fraying threads of doubt or confusion.

Ella imagined the knowing to either be a balmy, subtle peacefulness or a static-electric shock of hot pain. She had felt that before, at least—the physical jolt; the fast-jerk reflex of her hand; the raw cry punched from her throat. An answer, scorching and brief, without trying for it.

But Ella had never felt any balm, or any live-wire shocks of revelation. Impulsively wanting the thing in the rock hole had been about the closest she'd ever come to clarity. Her life questions hung, interminably, like damp sheets on an old rope line. Hack hung there, too. She thought she loved him, but some days she didn't really know.

Ella talked to Dr. North about it all. She sat on her therapist's couch, year after year, picking at the ruffles on the flowered cotton pillows as if the answer lay buried beneath the fabric. The older woman watched her—her blue eyes kind but searching; her voice soft yet probing.

"What do you really want, Ella?" the doctor asked once, a long time ago. Ella remembered looking at the tall woman with the long ponytail in casual, chic clothes; sitting in her leather recliner with her feet propped up, sandals on. "Do you want to finish school? Try not to think about it in terms of what you want right now, because the truth is, sometimes none of us ever knows."

"So how am I supposed to think of it, then?"

Dr. North smiled, her eyes crinkling at the edges. "Think of how you see yourself later. If you quit, where do you think that'll take you?"

Ella didn't hesitate. "Hopefully far away from here. Maybe the Peace Corps. Or California."

"I meant inside you. How do you think it'll make you feel about you?"

Ella picked pillow ruffles and pulled at her hair. She looked at the confident, pulled-together woman in front of her. "I don't know. Can't you just tell me what I should do?"

Dr. North laughed gently. "Of course I can't, Ella. I can only help you narrow down the options." Then she pushed down her footrest and leaned close, putting a hand over Ella's busy ones. She said seriously, softly, "I can't be your mother, honey. She's gone, and you have to figure out a way to do this yourself."

Ella had broken down, completely, for the first time. She sobbed for a long time. Dr. North held her hand.

Finally, Ella said, "I don't even know who I am. How am I supposed to know the answers?"

Dr. North was sympathetic. "It's hard to know who you are when you don't have memories of your own mother. She would have been your sense of origin; your anchor to the world. Knowing where you come from grounds you." She offered Ella tissues. "It gives you more confidence in yourself and your choices."

The doctor thought that if Ella had grown up with her mother, that if cancer hadn't killed her, Ella might have chosen to stay in school, or maybe she would have known well enough not to try it in the first place.

Ella, of course, was ambivalent about the analysis. She didn't quite see how the death of a mother she'd never known affected anything at all. But at least she cared enough to keep seeing her doctor all these years, and to hope for her mind to tell her, *Well, it's this or it's that, because if she died, I could die tomorrow. Better get on with things.*

But so far it hadn't happened.

"I'm trying the moleskin bandages," Hack said, bringing her back to the moment. "Then maybe I can pull on your arm harder, not scratch you up too much." He stood and pulled off his outer coat shell, dug in a pocket for the moleskin, and dropped the shell on the ground near Ella's free hand.

Ella watched him move, numb with cold and fear. "It won't work," she said levelly. "I'd need them on my hand, not my wrist." She looked at her wrist, trying to picture the hand attached to it. Maybe it was the cold, but she was starting to forget what her own hand looked like.

"Well I'm doing it anyway!" Hack barked. Furiously, he ripped open the square moleskin package, pulled out a handful of patches.

Ella shot him a look. Hack glanced at her and caught it. "Sorry." He tore off the bandage backing, then crouched down and patted the adhesive squares on Ella's wrist. "Just go through our coats and the packs and take out anything you think can help."

Ella shivered in the icy air. "Alright." With her free hand she rummaged through his shell and backpack, and her own pockets, then managed to finagle open her own pack, still hooked over her trapped arm. She threw everything on the snow at her feet, and found herself looking at a pile of water bottles, dried food pouches, energy bars, and hand and toe warmer packs. There were two tubes of lip balm and a compass/altimeter. A small lantern, a first aid kit, and a flint fire starter. Two knives. A fifty-foot bundle of 5/8" bull rope. And they had the tent and thermal sleeping bags, too.

Hack worked the moleskin wrap, smoothing it with care to Ella's wrist as if wet-casting a broken bone, even though, Ella thought, it was pointless. She saw him survey the contents of the gear pile; watched him grab the lip balm and pop the cap.

"What are you doing with that?"

"Grease," he said, eyes jetting to Ella's briefly and back to her wrist again. He slathered the wax around her wrist, now covered with the giant flesh-colored band-aid.

Panic took a deeper hold on Ella and her voice went shrill. "Hack, how's all this stuff on the outside of the hole going to help? My hand needs the wrap and the grease. My hand is inside the hole."

"Well we're not going to get inside until we try everything we've got." Hack held up the small tube. "And we've got grease."

Ella squirmed, anxiety filling her. "This is ridiculous! I can't believe you're wasting time with ChapStick!"

Hack spoke sternly, not looking at her, while he yanked on her arm. "I don't know, Ella. Maybe I just have a bad habit of trying to fix things that can't be reached."

Awkwardly, Ella wrenched her forearm out of Hack's hands and glared at him. "Yeah, well, I guess we all have our bad habits."

Hack dropped down and sat in the snow again. The flash of anger had warmed Ella briefly, carried her up and away from fear for a moment. She looked at Hack and he returned her gaze, but his eyes, half-hidden behind his shaggy blond hair, were unreadable.

Eventually, he spoke. "What were you thinking, anyway?"

Ella sighed heavily and put her head in her free hand. "That's the thing. I wasn't thinking. I did it before I even knew what I was doing." She laughed, mirthless. "Dr. North would have a heyday with that answer."

It was true. Ella could hear her doctor as if the woman was right next to her: This is a breakthrough, Ella. A sign. She'd probably even throw in something spiritual since she'd been doing that lately. Perhaps it was your mother helping you find a strong feeling; telling you to grab hold of something and move forward.

Ella snapped her head up, feeling a wave of chill run through her body. She shifted again, stretching her cramping legs out sideways. That left her right arm crossing her chest into the hole at shoulder height. She felt a pull to action and scanned the pile of supplies.

She focused on the knives. Hers was the Leatherman Crater 55B with a three-inch blade and four tools—all but the can opener, Ella thought, might be useful. Hack's BlackHawk CQD Mark 1 Type E Tactical knife—advertised as the "ultimate lifesaving tool," which had prompted Ella to buy it for his birthday—was more about survival.

Oh God, what if? Ella quickly pushed away the germ of mortal fear. Left handed, she picked up the BlackHawk and offered it to Hack.

"Can you chisel me out?"

Hack was facing the woods; he turned back with a jerk, his eyes wide. "Are you kidding me? With your hand wedged in that tight against icy rock? I'd slip for sure, and it wouldn't be good." He waved the knife away. "I'd rather you do it yourself, if that's what you want."

Ella dropped the BlackHawk in her lap and scoffed. "Left handed? I can't do anything left handed; much less operate on a rock wall."

They were silent another moment.

Then Hack said, "Give me the Leatherman."

Ella whipped her face toward him. "I thought you said—"

"—the blade's not as big on yours. Just hand it to me."

Ella reached over and grabbed it, tossed it to Hack. She sat motionless as he covered her trapped hand with his own gloved hand to shield her from a slip of the knife blade. Quickly, he took a deep breath and began chopping away at the edge of the rock hole, rapid-fire. Ella shuddered at the sound of the pinging stabs on unrelenting stone; at the image of the knife jamming through Hack's hand and into hers. Her heart thundered and breath wouldn't come. A wave of nausea slammed into her. In seconds, she threw her left hand around and grabbed Hack's stabbing arm.

"Stop! Stop! You're gonna cut me!"

Hack dropped the knife immediately.

"Jesus Christ!" Ella heaved several breaths in and out. She tried to calm down, looked at the pile of tools again. They swam before her eyes.

"The rope," she said, still breathing hard. "Try... the rope."

Hack looked dazed. Finally, he said, "I don't think the rope's going to do it."

Ella felt a surge of energy. Calmer, she picked up the nylon bull rope and tossed it to him. "Let's just try it."

She shifted again, her bottom freezing. She pulled her legs in front of her, bent her knees and braced her boots against the wall, in a birthing position of sorts, to push when Hack pulled. She pushed her hair, matted with sweat, off of her cheeks. Hack made a slipknot around her wrist and quadrupled the rope, giving it more girth. He inspected it, then re-inspected.

Ella's stomach lurched. "Hack." He turned to her. "Please don't break my hand."

In answer, Hack clenched his jaw. Ella tensed, fought another wave of nausea.

"On three," Hack said. He cleared his throat. "Try hard."

At this, Ella's body slackened. She turned sideways and looked at him where he stood, braced to pull.

"What's that supposed to mean, 'try hard'? Like I wouldn't?" Ella sputtered, channeling fear, anger, guilt. "I assume you're going to try hard because I'm afraid you'll break my hand. You don't assume I'll try hard? It's MY HAND in the rock!"

The rope went slack. Hack stepped away. "It didn't mean anything, Ella. They're just words that came out."

"They were NOT!" Ella shouted through chattering teeth. "Tell me what you meant!"

"Nothing."

"Tell me!"

"Just...choose to pull, is all I'm saying."

Ella's face grew mad-hot. "So, there it is, then. Just because you asked and I didn't choose yet because I needed some time. That's what this is all about."

Hack sighed and tightened the rope slightly. "Jesus, Ella. Do you really want to talk about this here, for God's sake? We're three days up the mountain and it's seven degrees. Just pull."

The raw facts quelled Ella's anger somewhat, but inflamed her panic. Her lungs lost their rhythm, and she couldn't reach any air. She vaguely heard Hack's three-count, but felt the rope tighten around her wrist as he pulled. Again, for a second, she thought she felt something in the hole. But Hack was pulling and Ella stopped thinking and pulled with him, leaning her hand into the rope to cushion the strain. The rope dug into her skin; she squeezed her palm pads together inside the hole, tried to mold her thumb into her fingers to lead her hand back out. Hack pulled harder. Pain shot through her palm, up her wrist, and she cried out.

"You dislocated my thumb!"

"What?"

"My thumb! You pulled too hard!"

Hack cursed loudly and dropped the rope. He fell to his knees, took her forearm gently in his hands and felt it for an obvious break. She leaned her forehead on his arm as he worked, tried to calm her jagged breathing. Counted to what seemed like a thousand. Hot tears ran down her cheeks.

Hack pulled her sleeves down over her exposed arm and held her.

Ella collapsed into a sob. "I'm gonna die here, Hack. I'm gonna die. And I wasn't even sure I wanted to come."

Hack pressed his lips to her cheek. "No one's dying." He paused. "I'm sorry. I shouldn't have pushed the trip. And I shouldn't have pulled so hard."

"I don't trust myself," she said, to his chest. "It's better when you lead."

Ella began to think, in this—of all places—that maybe Dr. North was right. Maybe she really did have no sense of origin, no feeling of place in the world—whether it was because she never knew her mother or because she was just crazy. She thought maybe she'd be better off just letting someone take care of her. Hack clearly wanted to do that. Why not just let him?

"I'm freezing, tired, and scared to death, Hack. Just tell me what to do."

Hack stared into her eyes, and it calmed her. "Okay, I don't like this, but here it is: the safety flare gun's not here and we had it at camp. Unless it's still in one of our packs, I'm gonna have to go back for it."

Ella had known it all along; she hadn't thrown it in the supply pile. "The packs are empty," she whispered.

"Then we dropped it or left it at the campsite. I need to go back and find it." Hack held her chin up, intense. "We need it, Ella."

"I know."

Hack moved his hand and Ella's head spun so hard she had to put it between her bent knees and close her eyes. She heard Hack at work, pitching the tent next to her, unrolling her sleeping bag for cover, gathering wood. Striking flint. She felt the hot flame of a fire growing just two feet from her.

She mentally calculated how long he could be gone. Three hours to the old camp site. Three hours back. She could hardly feel her trapped hand at all anymore. She wondered if, in six hours, she'd know she had a hand at all.

As Hack stacked firewood and food packs next to her, Ella's mind went to her doctor, her mother. What did she know of her mother? Nothing. No one ever told her anything. She had always felt like a ghost—come from nowhere, going nowhere. She couldn't even picture a face. How could she think of her mother if there was no face to attach to her? Both of them, just ghosts...

"Ella!" Hack shook her shoulder hard. "Are you alright?"

Ella looked up. Hack's eyes were full of fear. Her head had stopped spinning, but her mind was crumbling. She tried to hide it from him.

"I'm fine." She looked around at all he had done to protect her and then up at the late afternoon sky. "I'm tired. I'll eat something and then sleep, don't worry." She smiled slightly. "Thanks for the fire."

Hack pulled her hat down over her ears and forehead; pressed it tight to warm her. He put the Leatherman knife in her lap with the BlackHawk, then kissed her fast and stood.

"It won't be six hours, Ella. I promise."

Ella turned herself around as far as she could, hugging herself around the neck with her trapped arm to watch Hack quickly walk off. He didn't look back. Ella listened to the crunch of his boots in the snow until the sound faded. She stared out at the point where he disappeared, for how long she didn't know. *I'm going to die here*, she thought again. She tried to hold Hack's image in her unraveling mind.

She stared after him until her arm ached and she turned herself sideways again. She propped her trapped arm against the wall, now hot from the nearby fire. She stretched out her trapped fingers again and flexed them, trying to move the blood.

Then, she felt something inside the dark hole in the wall brush her fingers, again. And like before, Ella didn't feel cold stone. She didn't feel shiny metal or glass. She felt something that was alive.

She opened her mouth to scream, but the sound died in her throat. Because in the heat from the blazing fire, and amidst the spinning terror in her mind, Ella passed out.

***

She has the sense of drowning in darkness, but not dying. She is encased in water, and naked, though she has no sense of her stomach, breasts, thighs. Naked but warm. Water flows through her nose and mouth and lungs but she can breathe as if it is air. She is blind in darkness, cannot see; cannot move her arms or legs. She has the sense of being upside down but not dizzy, and curled in a tight ball. Hot waves of water undulate around her, lulling, comforting. Somehow, she reaches out a hand and her fingers graze a pulsing wall around her, a hot muscle that does not burn. She rests her hand there, in blindness, absorbing the rhythm, the heartbeat. It is rapture.

Then suddenly, she descends, turns so that she is facing completely the other side, opposite where she was. Water rushes around her, flowing fast. She feels something long and warm touch her hand, a rope maybe? But not like the rope Hack used on her wrist. She grabs it, holds on. It's long, Ella feels it could stretch for miles, does stretch for miles. It could take her far away from here, but she doesn't want to go. She's not afraid.

The water rushes forcefully now, in torrents. It leaves her bare skin against the hot, heaving walls around her. But it's painless. White light peeks in and Ella senses being squeezed, crushed, as if the walls are steel vices cranking closed around her. But still, there's no pain. She moves down slowly, sees brighter light, though her eyes are not open.

Then there are voices, screams. Her head is pulled viciously from the warm cave with a cold, plastic suction and her mouth and nose are in frigid air. She struggles for air, but why, when she knows how to breathe? Cold rubber is jammed up her nose and there is more suction; then air rushes in and she can breathe it as she was breathing the water just moments earlier. The suction goes in her mouth. She feels a wet mass pulled out, but she cannot inhale because the vice still has her lungs.

"Push!" a male voice says. "One more push!"

"I can't... I can't... do it," gasps a woman.

"You can. Try hard now. PUSH!"

And then Ella's shoulders emerge from the cave, pulsed out, and hands grab her shoulders and pull and her belly, legs, feet emerge too, and the air is frigid once again but she can expand her lungs and feel a breath move in and out of her body and cry out. She can only cry. She cries until she is wrapped in a blanket and placed on something warm and breathless; a chest? Then the blanket is pulled back and she feels hot, sweaty skin on her small body and cool, sweet breath on her face.

"Hello, my girl," the woman says, and Ella drowns, not in water, but in warm hands and bare breasts pillowing her head; in kisses on her cheeks and the crown of her head; in hot lips whispering her name over and over.

***

Ella awoke with a jerk, drenched and panting. She lay on the ground with her head against the rock, trapped arm up and across her face, looking at the sky. It was bright with the stream of the flares Hack had shot into the night sky.

She pulled herself up, leaned against the rock. She couldn't feel her right hand at all. For all she knew, it was already gone.

Hack stood before her, staring. Something in his eyes said he knew that Ella was not the same.

With a scorching gaze and flaming heart, Ella tried to tell Hack silently what she couldn't find the words to say. That she had finally felt the ground under her feet. That she'd grabbed the rope that tied her to life.

Ella shifted her cramped body for the last time. She sat upright, stretched her right arm out to its full length from her shoulder to the wrist held fast in the unforgiving rock.

The thought welled up in her mind—clear and sharp and doubtless. So loud that Ella thought she had spoken it to Hack.

Cut it off.

Ella picked up the BlackHawk and pushed it into his hand.

KILLING MOTHER
By Kim Younkin

The laminate on the rounded corners of the oblong metal
table I sit at has separated from the glue; I pick at its jagged
pieces with my left hand and twirl a black Rollerball with my
right, staring at the blank notepad in front of me. In this dank
room where clouds of cigarette smoke and stale coffee hang
heavy and rain down their stink, I am expected to scrawl words
confessing that I killed my mother.

They're there, behind wall-width, tinted interrogation
windows, watching. They think I can't see their bug-eyed,
leathery faces, enduringly scarlet and sagging from drink; their
sour breath fogging the glass; their wilted self-esteem. They
think I can't hear them call me a "freak" and a "waste," and
laugh at my cropped hair and black clothes, like everyone has
always done, all my life.

But I can see and hear it all. Even things others can't.

The tall one among the three, with the dimpled stomach
that swells against a drab, threadbare sport coat, is Andy. He
and his pals know I was there when my mother died, that my
gun killed her. They know my clothes are stained with her
blood, heard my voice on the 911 tape calling to report "an
accident." They thought wringing a statement from me would
be a cinch, so they sent in Andy. I'm a short, slight woman.
Easy prey, so they think.

In Andy's first barrage of questions, I answered none to
his liking—four, I purposely answered before he asked.

Then, I trampled perfectly on his words with the answer,
"We didn't have one," as he opened his mouth and asked, "What
was your relationship with your mother like?"

That spooked him. He got flustered and turned on the

intimidation, then left me to take a "break" so I could "just think about that, sweetheart." As if I had clicked him here from prime time television with my remote control.

Now he paces behind the glass with the other two, watching me with a mixture of lurid anticipation and mild confusion as I roll the pen, a baton between my fingers. Beads of sweat form on his brow as he imagines the places he could go if he breaks me.

He turns his back to the window and I release the pen. It continues to twirl freely in the air in front of me. The other two jerks behind the glass see it and gape—long enough for them to stop calling me names—but neither has enough guts to look at the other. I take it back into my hand quickly, hoping it makes them wonder if they really saw that they think they did.

I will not admit guilt, become a sideshow in the legal circus, rot in a cell. Nor will I live at the women's correctional facility, breathing in iron ore from the neighboring steel plant and laundering menses stains out of the panties of man-women for twenty years to life.

I'm done with imprisonment.

I pick up the pen, furrow my brow as if crafting my admission, and write in large capital letters on the yellow paper, "A-N-D-Y." I tear it from the pad with a flourish and hold it up to face the tinted window. Their whispered, collective "Ah, shit" pierces the glass wall between us as if it were a missile, searing my eardrums, and I press my hands quickly to my ears, grunting softly.

I fold my hands on my lap as the door opens.

Andy's belly comes in first, then his pudgy, ham-sized fist clenched tightly around a tattered, paper coffee cup with teeth marks around the rim; then he ducks his head through the doorframe and hauls in the rest of his bulk.

"What?" he says rudely, parking in front of me, mid-step.

"There's only me in here. Why do you need them?" I

ask with a wide, sweet smile.

"What are you talking about?"

I nod toward the window. "Your friends."

Andy spins around to survey the tint for chinks. Seeing none, he says, "Who says there's anyone else in there?"

"Oh, Andy. Please," I say, rolling my eyes.

"Detective Holmes," he growls.

I ignore him and look at the glass, wink at the other two inside, then look back to Andy. I point to the chewed cup. "Looks like I make you a little nervous." I sit back in my seat and smugly cross my arms over my chest. "Had to call for reinforcements, huh?"

He glares at me hard and thumps the cup down on the table, splashing a drip of cold coffee on my writing hand. Then he pulls out the chair opposite me, its unpadded feet screeching across the tile floor, and drops his girth on the seat.

"I can sit here, or I can sit back there," he says, eyes narrowed. "It doesn't make a bit of difference to me. You look pretty screwed either way."

"Yes. Well…" I pick up the pen and point it at the window as if it's a fairy godmother's wand. I draw a circle around the men inside once, twice—voila!—then lower it and slide it across the table to Andy.

"I think this is yours."

"That's a bad move." His eyes are dark, his voice grave. He wrinkles his brow and stares at me hard.

"I don't think you should try to scare me, Andy."

"So why won't you sign?"

"It's very complicated, as I've said."

"And as I've asked, many times, what happened with your mother?"

I lean forward and meet his gaze, unflinching. "Maybe," I say slowly, "you should call your wife back first. I'll sit here and wait for my lawyer."

54

Andy's eyebrows shoot up to his hairline and he stares at me quizzically.

"How the fu—?" he tries to get out, but his words drown in the sound of a mammoth crash from behind the viewing window.

He whips his head around—as if, like me, he could see what's happening in there—then turns back to me, his face crimson and bulging. "Sit tight," he says through clenched teeth, then pushes to his feet and exits the room.

"Of course, Andy."

His red face conjures the memory of telling Mother about the voices in my head. A scorching wave of lava-colored anger flowed up her graceful neck and filled her face when, two years before, I finally, desperately, begged her for help.

"They sneer at me, Mother," I choked, the strength of my sobs forcing spit from my mouth. "They make me hurt myself."

Her head had seemed an orb of orange flames, her eyes afire as I told her how, sometimes, I could read people's minds, make salt shakers move just by looking at them. A touch to her hot, furious cheek then might have wounded me as I can wound; might have burned the prints from my fingers, rendered me unidentifiable.

She had spoken through a clamped jaw, just like Andy. It had looked wired shut.

"Lydia... Anne... Walker." In a black whisper, she rasped out my full name, criticizing, the way she had since I was seven—for using the wrong fork with my salad, addressing a formal guest informally, quietly reading a book on the "good" couch.

I had dropped to my knees and wrapped my arms around her nylon-covered calves, which stiffened when I touched her. Tears shot from my eyes as I cried for her to hold me.

"Mother. Mommy, please."

"You...," she had hissed through gritted teeth, "will

never speak… of this… again."

Then, she had yanked away from my grasp, turned on her lambskin pump. She summoned her driver and left me in the foyer of her penthouse, alone.

Next door to the room I'm in, a door slams open and into the wall behind it. Then, someone is yelling at someone else in the hall.

"How could it just blow up?!" says a deep male voice I can't match to a face.

"It's brand new!" shouts Andy. "How does a brand new camera just explode?!"

"What?!" The other man's voice is small in his defense. "I didn't do anything but turn it on. I didn't! Just move her to the other room!"

Then there's unintelligible shouting from the unnamed voice as the man walks down the hall, away from the room.

Short minutes pass, and Andy comes back in, still red-faced and sweating.

"So. Am I moving?" I ask, smiling.

"Cut the crap and answer my questions!" he booms. He treads around the table a few times, sits down hard in his chair, and takes two deep breaths. I can see nicotine stuck to his lungs.

I look over his shoulder at the window behind him, and, knowing there's no longer anyone there, I oblige.

"Well, you didn't ask me directly. You assumed. But I didn't kill her."

Andy exhales and rubs his temples. I feel sorry for him. "Then what is it? Are you gonna tell me you have a twin?" His voice is calmer.

I get up from my chair and walk away from the table toward the wall behind me.

"Sort of," I mutter under my breath, back turned to him, a smirk on my lips.

"What?"

I face him and lean against the wall, bending my right knee and propping the sole of my foot behind me. I cross my arms at my chest, and smirk more.

He stabs me with his eyes.

"No, I don't have a twin." I walk back to the table and bend down to meet his face.

I singsong, "But. YOU. Do!"

Andy's hot air balloon face looks as if I've popped it with a pin. He leans against the chair back and gawks at me, dumbfounded.

"A sister, right? Andy and Andrea." I cluck my tongue three times. "How suh-weet. Oh! Now that I think of it, your wife was actually calling about Andrea. What a coincidence that we're talking about her now!" Andy leaps from his chair as I say, "You really should call her back, you know."

His eyes narrow, a pinch of fear flitting through them. "Tell me who told you that."

"Gee, I hope nothing's wrong. Is something wrong? Are you waiting to hear any news?"

He leans toward me, hands outstretched, jaw clenched. "Shut. UP."

"Is she sick?" I ask in a low voice, eyebrows arched high, as he gets closer. "Is your little twin sister awfully, sadly sick?"

Andy lunges at me from where he stands, lands stomach down on the metal table between us. His weight rams the table into my chest, pinning me to my seat. He wraps his hands around my neck, squeezes.

I glare into his wild eyes, my own, unblinking, and choke, "My m-mother...k-killed...her...self."

His face is inches from mine. I see his madness, the veins in his forehead pulsing with hot blood and rage, burst blood vessels in the whites of his eyes. I smell the hate in the rivers of sweat that trickle from his brow, in the blistering breath rasping from his mouth.

I see what my mother must have seen in me, on the night she died.

My words stir him slightly and he pulls back, lets go of my throat. "It's your... gun," he pants. "Your prints... are on it." He remembers himself, jerks his hands off my throat. Clambers to his feet and walks backward toward the door. "You pointed it... at her head and fired."

I rub my neck with both hands and glower at him. "Yes. And no."

I tell Andy how, the night of my mother's death, I went to her penthouse apartment unannounced, interrupted her at her evening tea, literally—her cup was in her silk-gloved hands and perched at her lips when I entered the room. I brought a packed bag, asked her if I could stay. The voices were getting to me again, leaving me no room to breathe. I needed company, even if it was hers. She had declined, as always. She did it with her back turned to me, despite my wracking sobs.

I take a break from my story and make a sweeping motion with my arm toward where Andy is standing across the room from me. As I do, the other chair slides over to where he is.

"Need to sit down, Andy?"

Andy turns and grabs the door handle, but it's stuck.

"Open it, you damn FREAK!" he shouts.

I laugh. "That's what Mother called me!"

I tell Andy, as he stands at the door, how the gun I kept in my bag for protection spilled out as I fell upon the floor at my mother's feet, begging her to let me stay.

"But she walked away from me, a cold, unfeeling wake trailing behind her. And my hatred just followed her. It was amazing, really. I had no idea, then, what I could do with hatred. My gun just followed her. Followed her all the way to swinging kitchen door and nuzzled right up to her head. It

58

didn't take long to figure out what I could make the trigger do."

Andy frantically turns the door handle, ashen.

"She tried to pry it off her temple, but it didn't work." I shrug mockingly. "Oops!"

Andy looks down in horror as the lock strap that holds his 45 magnum in place on his belt opens and his gun comes out, of its own volition, and raises itself to his head. He tries to grab his gun. But of course, he can't. He's a weakling just like the rest.

"It was sort of like that," I say flatly.

Andy's eyes close and he presses his back to the door behind him, his trembling palms to his thighs.

"Okay," he says, his breathing ragged, sweat coursing down his face so fast now that it dampens the neckline of his collared shirt. "Jesus Christ. Okay."

"Is it ever really okay, Andy?"

He nods his head. "Okay! ALRIGHT!"

"Do you promise me? Please say you promise."

"Yes," he croaks. "I promise."

I smile broadly, eye the gun back to its holster. Click the lock strap.

"Why thank you, Andy." I say it as if I have known him for years, as if he has performed a kind, neighborly task, like picking up my mail while I was away.

Just then, the door opens easily, and in walks my lawyer, her long skirt rustling around her fat ankles.

I look up at her in greeting, a sweet smile on my face, while Andy slumps into the chair.

"Rita," I say slowly. "I believe I no longer need your services."

Amy Dalrymple

Amy Dalrymple is originally from Milwaukee, Wisconsin and now lives in Columbus, Ohio.

She studied philosophy at The Ohio State University. "A Practical Guide for Feeding Captive Children" is her first published story.

For more information, please visit www.amydalrymple.com.

This work proudly presented by the following sponsor

Le Pooch Luxury Dog Walking & Pet Services

Providing luxury pet services to Columbus, Ohio and its surrounding communities.

www.LePooch.net

A PRACTICAL GUIDE
FOR FEEDING CAPTIVE CHILDREN
By Amy Dalrymple

The captive child must be contained. This containment may be physical, e.g. a kind of lock or cage, or psychological, e.g. inducing fear of harm.

The first night, I slept underneath the Main Street Bridge. No, that's not right. I did not sleep. I crouched underneath the Main Street Bridge, seeking shelter from rain that poured down in sheets. It was that cold and piercing rain of early spring, and it stabbed my bare skin, my face and hands, and it shattered like broken glass, like broken liquor bottles when it hit the ground. It echoed in the space beneath the bridge, a horrible screeching sound in my ears, in my head, until I could not bear it anymore.

My heart pounded the whole time. It was too obvious a place for a teenage runaway. They won't find me, I told myself consolingly over and over. They are all asleep, and they won't miss me until morning, or maybe if I'm lucky until after school—unless—unless he comes to my room tonight. My stepfather.

When he crept into my room, I thought of other things, like particle physics, but I kept my eyes open, and I made mandalas on my bedroom ceiling.

I had gotten slightly into Buddhism, but I did not talk about it with my mom, or anyone. It was just one more thing in a long list of secrets.

I left the bridge before the rain stopped, but it had at least slowed a little. I began walking toward downtown, zig-zagging down side streets. These streets were dark, and I was afraid, but I did not want to risk being discovered on the busier roads.

I had a bus ticket to Blue City in my backpack. I bought it ahead of time to be certain I would not arouse suspicion or be asked for ID. The bus would depart at 4:35 a.m. I did not want to arrive too early, but I would make good time walking.

I had packed light. I left nearly everything behind. All that I had was now in my backpack—two changes of clothing, a few necessary toiletries, only one book—my old copy of *A Brief History of Time*, given to me by my father when I was only seven, protected by two gallon-size Ziploc bags.

I left a note in my bedroom, even though I did not want to. I wanted to leave no trace, but I worried that they would think I was kidnapped. I hoped that the police would take my case less seriously, since I was almost 18. Maybe they would let me slip through the cracks, slip away.

I had never in my life been this afraid, not even the first time my stepfather touched me. But that was a different kind of fear.

I was sad for leaving my mom and my baby sister. I loved them, and this was not their fault. They would not understand. They had been my whole reason for living. I tried not to worry about my baby sister. I told myself that he did not like children, that he preferred young women who had matured but who could not fight back. I told myself that he would not harm his *own* daughter. I hoped these things were true, because I could not save her.

I slipped my wrist out of the sleeve of my sweatshirt and unclasped my sterling silver charm bracelet. My mom had given it to me in seventh grade. The first charm was a heart with my name engraved on it, Matilda. I gripped it in my fist as I walked, until my hand became too sweaty. Then I stopped and clasped it back around my wrist.

The rain finally stopped just as I approached downtown. I guessed I had been walking for a little more than an hour. The bus station was close now, only a few blocks away. I began to cry, softly. I could not help it. What had I done? I had set something in motion, and now I could not turn back.

Even worse, at the last moment before I left, out of impulsive anger, I had emptied his stash of liquor, poured each bottle down the kitchen sink, left them sitting on the counter. His rage was all too real to me; I could almost hear it, feel it, and now I regretted what I had done. What if he found it before I reached the bus and came after me? What if he found me? From then on, I expected him to creep up behind me at any moment. Everything would be over.

I was a good girl from the suburbs. Despite my pain, despite my own private hell, I had no street skills. I had an allowance and an iPhone and a Starbucks card. But I didn't want those things anymore. I could no longer be kept like a caged animal, like a reptile that serves no purpose other than to be brought out, petted, and harassed upon occasion for the amusement of its owner. I was free from him now, as long as I did not get caught. But I was on the streets, too, and I did not know how to survive here.

The bus. Despite my worries, no one expressed suspicion of my age. Waiting outside the terminal to board, I stood on the concrete and stared at my reflection in a big puddle of rainwater, illuminated by yellow streetlight. My long brown hair—same as my dad's—curly and wild from the rain, my face pale and ashen from cold and fear, my eyes just a dark glimmer in the water. Just a reflection, a shade of a girl I did not recognize and did not wish to see. I stomped in the puddle with my right sneaker, and the water went all the way to my ankle, but I didn't care because my feet were already soaked.

The bus driver motioned for us to board. Few other people were traveling at that hour, and I shared the bus with only a handful of other passengers. We lined up to deposit our luggage outside the bus before we filed on. The man in front of me was ragged in torn jeans and a dirty sweatshirt, and he smelled of alcohol. He motioned for me to board ahead of him—ladies first—so I had to smile, but I was afraid of him, and I hoped he would not sit near me. I chose a seat near the front, resting my head against the cold window. There was no turning back now. Things were out of control. I was traveling at 70 miles per hour, for the first time toward something unrecognizable.

Outside, it was pouring again. I drifted in and out of sleep, my dreams strange and unsettling. I dreamed of my father. My father, gone for nearly five years now. I was twelve when he died. An aneurism in his heart. He didn't know about it; no one did. One day he was with us, happy and well, the next day, gone.

Gone, gone, gone.

When I was little and rambunctious, sometimes he would bring me with him to the university where he taught, to get me out of my mother's hair. Sometimes he even let me skip school when I wasn't sick to tag along with him. He spent a lot of time in his office, at his computer, or scribbling long equations at the big, green chalkboard that took up a whole wall. His colleagues—the other physics graduate students—spoiled me with peanut butter cookies and hot chocolate from the dining hall.

I liked his classroom best. My dad was a magician,

sort of. He set fires and pulled white linen tablecloths out from under full sets of dishes, demonstrating principles of heat or motion, trying to hold his students' interest. Oh, I loved it, and I wondered if my mom knew about the magic, or if it was a secret, just between us.

My dad and his colleagues taught me things I was much too young to understand. They talked to me as if I were much older, perhaps one of their students.

"Time behaves in strange ways. For instance, you go to school for seven hours each day, but some days that seven hours goes by very quickly, if you're having fun, and other days— maybe if you're excited to come home because we are going out for pizza or leaving for a trip—that same seven hours lasts a long time."

I understood this. Some of the other things they told me went above my head, but I carried them around with me, like mantras, repeated them in my mind and sometimes out loud, until I was old enough to understand.

"Time is slippery and weird. It twists and turns and bends in ways we don't expect it to, and don't really understand. The beautiful thing is that all kinds of things are possible, absurd things."

And even though my dad died, and even though I don't get to go to the university anymore, he still talks to me; the other physicists keep me company.

I wanted to be a physicist like my dad. I had the talent; my mom bragged about me sometimes. She told people that I had inherited the physics gene. But I didn't really think so. I studied hard, and why not, I had little else to entertain me. No friends, no life. So I buried myself in books, and I took advanced math classes, and twice a week I got out of high school early to attend a physics course at the community college. I liked math and physics best because I could always find an answer.

April. I was going to Blue City for April, and no one else. I met her at an Alateen meeting. It seemed like so long ago. She had moved to the Blue City with her boyfriend last summer. Before she left, we had coffee. She squeezed my hand.

"Matilda, if you ever need anything, if you ever need a place to stay, I'm here. Please call me."

Now, I was coming to Blue City, to April. Maybe it wasn't far enough away, three hours by bus or car. It was a start, though. And I hoped they would not expect to find me there. But I had not called ahead. I was too afraid I would be caught. Or that April might say no, and then I would lose my nerve, stay. I hoped she could help me. I had nowhere else to go.

The child's basic needs must be provided for, such as food, shelter, adequate heat, and nourishment. Socialization, however, should be discouraged.

My first Alateen meeting. There were fliers on the bulletin board at Starbucks, fluorescent yellow to grab our attention, I guess. *Is someone's drinking bothering you? Alateen is for you. Alateen is for young people whose lives have been affected by someone else's drinking.*

I pulled one off the board one day, quickly and surreptitiously. I did not know who was watching, who would wonder.

My circumstances were murky, undefinable. Was my stepfather an alcoholic? I didn't know. I knew he smelled of liquor when he crept into my bedroom. I knew he hid his bottles, but he didn't drink every day. He fought with my mother occasionally, and sometimes violently. Maybe she could let it slide because it happened rarely, two or three times a year. And if we were careful, if we tread lightly and did not anger him, things might be okay. I don't know how he could have hidden his occasional nighttime absences from her, but I had to believe that she did not know.

I crumpled the flier and tossed it into the trash can before going into the church. My hands were shaking as I opened the big wooden door. I was always shaking. Inside, the lobby was dim and silent. The meeting was in the basement, I knew, but I just stood in the lobby for a moment, alone, breathing deeply.

What was I doing here? Could I really walk down the stairs, into a room full of strangers? I almost chickened out, and I turned around to leave, when the door opened, and two girls I did not recognize walked in. They both smiled at me as they walked by.

"Are you coming?" one of them asked me, kindly. Her invitation was just enough for me to convince myself not to turn back. I took another deep breath and followed them to the basement.

I did not speak at the meeting, other than to give my name. I did not speak much anywhere. School was terrifying. I couldn't have friends, because I had too many secrets, because I was so crippled with anxiety that I could not speak to my peers, because even if I had, I couldn't bring anyone back to that forsaken house. And my mom and stepfather would not have allowed me to go anywhere without knowing the people I was with, without meeting their parents. They wanted to *protect* me. But these people seemed nice. Maybe I could make a friend here, where everyone's home was probably kind of terrible, too.

A woman about my mom's age led the meeting. She had short hair and kind eyes. She seemed like the kind of person you could trust. She talked about God. God is an important part of the twelve step programs, she explained.

"But you don't have to believe in God to participate. Some people just believe in a higher power. You can use whatever name you like. That's why we say, 'God as we understood him'. We all understand God differently."

I shifted in my seat. This straightforward way of speaking made me uncomfortable.

She continued, "Sometimes, I like to imagine what God would look like, if he were a person. I'd like to start by doing that now, if that's okay with everyone."

It was.

"Good. Just close your eyes for a moment and think about what God would look like to you." I thought of Buddhism, the books I had been reading, the mandalas, but I could not picture any person or face.

But, when I closed my eyes, I was surprised. I saw a woman, but I did not know the origin of her image. She looked like no one I had met before, with long, curly hair, strawberry blond hair that dazzled in the sunlight, with soft, radiant skin. She had strong arms and gentle hands. I saw her reaching her hand for my own. I longed for her touch. I wished she could really hold me and make things right again.

I raised my right hand, my cold, white hand, and knocked. Hard. Once, twice, three times on April's door. It was a rickety old door, green paint peeling, a long walk from the bus station to a poor side of town.

I waited for a long time, biting the inside of my cheek so hard that it began to throb. I wanted to leave, but where would

I go? I was about to knock again when the green door opened, abruptly. It was a girl I did not recognize, a hippie girl with long blond dreadlocks and bright eyes, wearing a paisley gypsy skirt.

"Hi." She seemed friendly.

"I'm Matilda," I said. "I'm looking for April."

"Oh." The way she said it was not good. "Um—April's not here right now."

Tears welled up in my eyes, even though I tried to fight them. I had held my tears back so many times. My tears and my fear and my seething anger.

"Oh, honey." The girl stepped out onto the front stoop, and she put her arm around me, and she led me inside, into the living room, onto a beat-up old sofa, upholstered in a scratchy plaid fabric.

"April isn't here right now," she said again, softly. "She and Eric are just having a little fight right now, but she'll be back. They love each other."

I nodded. I sniffled. I couldn't speak.

"Are you in trouble?"

"Kind of."

"You need a place to stay." It was a statement, not a question. She knew. She sighed defeatedly.

"I wish I could help. I wish I could let you stay, but I don't even really live here. I'm just crashing, too."

My heart sank. I had assumed that she was confident and together. But her eyes seemed vulnerable, and her shoulders slumped a little, like she was tired and weary. April, too, I had thought to be more capable. She had a job and a boyfriend, and she went to school part-time. But now I realized these girls could not help me. Maybe they were just as lost as me.

"But I know April will let you sleep here when she comes back. Do you have her number?"

I shook my head. "I left my cell phone behind."

"I'll try to reach her for you. She hasn't been answering. She's just angry. Until then…" She paused, grabbed a notebook from the floor and a pen from her pocket, scribbled something on paper. She tore the page from the notebook and handed it to me—an address, a crude map.

"It's a sort of commune, an old factory down by the university. April and I stayed there for awhile. There's an attic; you can sleep there. They don't lock the doors, so you can get in pretty much anytime. But you should probably sneak in, at night."

She fretted over me a little before I left, offered me provisions, as much as I could carry: a sleeping bag, food, a knit hat, mittens, socks. This added considerably to my load, and the extra bags made me more conspicuous, but I was grateful.

"I'll try to do what I can. I'll try to come pick you up when April comes back. If anyone sees you, just act natural. Just act like you're supposed to be there, like you're someone's guest."

I nodded.

So, I went to the factory, an old knitting factory. I walked for hours before I found it, getting lost on unfamiliar streets. I stopped two or three times to rest, sitting on wet benches, and once at a funky hole-in-the-wall hotdog place where I felt dirty and unwelcome. I ate quickly and left. I did not have much cash, and I dared not use the credit card my mom had insisted I keep for emergencies. I knew that my purchases could be tracked. They could not find out that I was in Blue City.

The factory had another name, of course, but I did not know it. The artists and hippies and communists and anarchists who lived there had given it a name, but it was unmarked. It was not yet dark when I found it, so I left again.

I wandered aimlessly, killing time. The neighborhood was old and run-down, but interesting. The houses all had front porches, real porches, unlike the tiny whitewashed ones in our neighborhood that were just for show. These porches had swings and rocking chairs, and I imagined people wiling away their evenings, smoking and talking. It was still too cold for porch sitting, but when I glanced over my shoulder once I thought I saw someone wave to me from one of those porches, one of my dad's old physics friends, maybe, looking out for me.

I passed a corner store. Maybe I would go there in the mornings for coffee, in my new life. More shops—a barber shop, a pawn shop, restaurants. A school, in the Gothic style; it looked like a castle. I wished I could go to class there, make some friends. I grew weary, walking through this landscape as if it were a movie, as if I were not a part of it. The light began to fade, and the wind picked up; its whispers chilled me, haunted me, like his breath on my neck. What were the words?

I crossed an intersection, and as I stepped onto the sidewalk, I thought I saw movement out of the corner of my eye, the shadow of a man. I whipped my head around and saw a man in a dark coat and trilby hat disappearing into the doorway of a nondescript building. *Him*? My heart pounded. He wore a trilby to work each day, and a dark jacket, even in the summer. He was concerned with appearances.

Could he have found me already? Maybe I had not run far enough. Maybe I should get on another bus. I quickened my pace. Chills crept through my body; goose bumps covered my arms underneath my sweatshirt, my hands lost their color, turned gray. I could not stay outside any longer. I had to find a safer place.

I must have been getting closer to the university, because

I began to see more students. I passed two bookstores before finding a coffee shop where I sought shelter. I was wary of my luggage, but no one seemed to notice me. It was a hip place, where kids wore thrift-store clothes and didn't wash their hair and scribbled in black notebooks. They seemed almost as weird as me. My heart was racing, so I drank green tea instead of coffee. When night fell, I made my way back to the factory.

Up three flights of stairs, the third rickety and scary, to the attic, dark and deserted. I had a small key-chain flashlight and nothing else to illuminate that darkness. I searched for a long time to find a good spot in the attic. It had to be quiet, and far from the door. Not too dark, not too cold. The spring nights were often frigid, and they would be even more so now that I was near the lake. The floorboards were rotted and often missing, and I had to step carefully.

Finally, I settled on a spot. I immediately put on my hat and mittens and socks, and I got into the sleeping bag, and I ate the first food I retrieved from my backpack—a banana, a can of baked beans, a Snickers bar. Then I slept.

I awoke with a start the next morning, surprised and confused for a moment by my strange surroundings. Until I remembered. My chest felt heavy again. Would it always feel like this? Light poured into the attic from tall windows on all four walls. The sunlight illuminated the ruinous attic, crumbling wood and broken glass, cobwebs and assorted beer bottles, remnants of other exiles.

It was a pitiful and bereft place, this attic, so I painted it with silver, and I lay awake in my sleeping bag for a long time, my eyes dazzled by the shining light.

The child's diet should be healthful and well-balanced, but care should be taken to ensure that the child does not become too stimulated or vigorous. The captive child will be easier to control if she is lethargic and apathetic.

The days passed in the attic. During the day I hid, as much as I could anyway. I read *A Brief History of Time* a few times. I read old newspapers. I thought of trying to get a library card, but I was afraid that I would get into trouble, somehow. I tried not to drink, so I would not have to pee. If I did, I sneaked quickly, quietly through the corridors. On the few occasions when I ran into other people in the factory, I acted "natural", as April's friend instructed. Nothing happened. No one caught me. Yet.

Sometimes, during moments when I was not completely absorbed by fear, I grew bored. It was a feeling I had rarely experienced in my previous life. I had little to stave off my boredom, so I began exploring the attic, careful not to make much noise. It was one big, open room, and other than some trash that others had left behind and my few belongings, it was mostly empty. There was some spare lumber, old and rotted and probably useless, a pile of storm windows and extra screens, and some random bits of metal and other parts I did not recognize.

But the best discovery was the missing floorboards. In three places, there were holes through which I could see the floor below me. Only one of them provided any real view, and I had to lie on the floor and press my face against the hole, but I could see. I was grateful that this hole afforded a view of the corridor and not someone's loft, which would have been too creepy.

Long hours passed as I lay sprawled on my stomach, waiting for people to come and go. Mostly, I was disappointed.

There was far less movement than I hoped for. I did not see people often enough to recognize anyone, or to determine who actually lived there. A girl, about my age, with frizzy hair, who I saw and then heard knocking on a door outside of my view. An older man with a scruffy beard.

And then, one evening, when the light was almost too dim for me to see, *a man in dark clothing, wearing a trilby.* He was following me. He must know where I am, then, but why had he not come for me? Was he psyching me out? Was he trying to make me crazy with fear before he came to retrieve me? I wanted to run away, but I remained frozen in place, watching. I heard a door shut, and I watched for as long as I could, until it was much too dark to see anything at all.

April did not come. Her friend with the dreads had promised to send her as soon as she returned, and I waited and waited, knowing eventually she would arrive, but she did not. I lost track of time. I left the factory when I could, when I thought it was safe, to use the restroom, to buy food. It must have been a week before I dared take a shower in one of the communal bathrooms. A few days more, and already my cash was running low, and still April did not come. She was not going to. We were not close friends. She was just a nice girl from Alateen who had made an offer to help once, and it was clear that she could not help. Maybe she was in trouble like me.

My anxiety grew. Things were really getting out of control now. What could I do? What should I do? I could not return to my mother and stepfather's. Seven months, I told myself, only seven months until my eighteenth birthday, salvation. Surely I could not starve in seven months' time. Surely I could survive, somehow. Even if I had to leave the factory, I could survive. But I tried not to think of that.

I tried meditating, I tried lying to myself—it will be okay—I tried to summon my dad and the comforting words he might whisper, but I knew it was useless. I had to wait until he showed up on his own.

I began to feel so lonesome that it hurt me physically, like I had been punched in my stomach. I missed my mom and my baby sister. I brought only a few photographs with me, and I took them from my wallet and looked at them over and over again. I touched them, like you aren't supposed to do, traced their faces, their bodies with my finger.

My father, at least, kept me company. My father and the physicists. I no longer tried to convince myself that they did not exist. I no longer told myself they were false visions —hallucinations—I must conceal from others. I was good at concealing things, and I was good at reason, but I was so weary of deception, and so lonesome, so I stopped fighting.

Mostly, they gave me physics lessons, like the old days.

"Hey, kiddo, want to see a neat trick?"

And, like a dream, I would remember some demonstration. Centrifugal force. One of them filled a bucket with water, and swung it in giant arm-circles, the water remaining inside the bucket. After I was convinced, the bucket was abandoned and forgotten, until my dad tripped and knocked the bucket over, spilling the water. Intent on their words, I forgot the spilled water, until I scuffled shoeless across the attic and stepped in a puddle. I cried out, startled, confused. The words dissipated, like always. I was alone, and the water was probably just from the leaky roof, a light rain the night before.

But there were more than just physics lessons. In my ruinous attic, my father spoke to me as if he had never gone, as if the past that stretched from his death until this day had never happened. He spoke to me as if we were just sitting at the kitchen table, eating our eggs sunny-side up.

The child must be *controlled*. A state of constant anxiety is necessary to ensure that the captive child remains psychologically weak and unable to fight or to flee.

Sometimes I left the factory late at night. It was probably dangerous and stupid, but I would get this reckless feeling, and I had to *go*. The city was different in the dead of night, almost as if it was not the same city at all. At first I expected to see other late night wanderers, but usually I was alone. Once, a cop car even drove up really close, and my heart thumped and raced. The car rolled to a stop, and I did not turn my head, but the officer called out to me, "Hey!"

I had no choice. I turned to him, walked up to the car. *It's over now*, I thought with doom. Even if I told my story, explained why I had run away, they could not protect me from him. I looked up at the officer, black haired beneath his hat, his eyes unexpectedly friendly. I waited, but said nothing.

"Are you lost? Do you know this is a rough neighborhood?"

He didn't know who I was. He was only trying to help.

"Yes, I know. I live here."

"I have a daughter about your age, and I wouldn't want her walking around alone this time of night. Do you need a ride somewhere?"

He seemed like a nice guy. I wished I could accept his offer. I wished I had somewhere that he could give me a ride *to*.

"No, thank you. I just can't sleep. I'm going home soon." The lie came so easily.

"Okay," he agreed hesitantly. He pulled the car away from the curb and yelled out as he drove off, "Be careful!"

My father and the physicists came along, usually. They talked to me about the things I had read during the day, wondrous things. *All kinds of things are possible. Absurd things.* They were silent, much of the time, but I was not sure they were not real. Time was slippery, weird, after all.

There were awful things, too, like the shadow man in the trilby. I could never figure out if it was him or not. I tried to tell myself it wasn't, that my imagination was out of control, but the fear remained all the same, followed me around in all my waking hours, more constant a companion than my dead father or the physicists.

The streets were dirty and wretched, like me; maybe that's why I liked them. And the quiet—I never imagined a big city could be so still. I saw and heard things you would never see in the daytime. I sat down right on the sidewalk, in front of a sleek glass building and watched a little bird hopping around, eating crumbs for a whole hour. I found things on the ground and I picked them up, because no one was watching. I saved some of these things. My favorite was a hot pink button, which I kept in my coat pocket with my spare change, and it made me feel better. I found a whole sandwich in its wrapper on the top of a trash bin, and I was so hungry, I ate it without thinking twice. It was tuna, but I figured it wasn't bad yet since it was still so cold outside.

One night, I woke to a thunderstorm. The sky was pitch-black. Most nights, the moonlight and the streetlights kept the attic from total darkness, but when I woke there were no streetlights, and it was so dark that I could scarcely make out my own body. Another deafening clap of thunder, and lightning streaked across the sky and I was frightened. I had to get out of the attic, if only to sit alone in some corridor of the factory, closer to other people.

I walked slowly, my arms reached out in front of me, my naked toes stretching out to explore the territory before me. I was making progress; I thought that I could make out the doorway, and I sashayed toward it, light on air like a ballet dancer.

Bang! Another clap of thunder. It startled me, and I lost my balance. I stumbled and could not catch myself, and as lightning flashed right outside the attic windows, searing pain shot through my right foot, and up my leg, and through my entire body. I fell to my knees.

When I tried to move my leg, to assess the damage, I discovered that it was stuck—I had stepped through a gap in the floor. Tears came to my eyes—all the tears I had not shed for all these days, all these years. I felt with my hands for my foot, and I pushed and pulled and tugged until my hands were scraped and bleeding, and my foot was freed. Immediately, I could tell that it was bleeding, too, and swelling.

I knew that I could not put weight on it. The attic was still pitch-black; I could not crawl or hop out. I would have to wait until morning. So I waited for the lightning, and each time it flashed, I memorized the scene in front of me, and I crawled, slowly, cautiously, until I found my sleeping bag. I lay awake, motionless, for a long, long time.

Finally, my father began to whisper in my ear. "It's okay, it's okay." I fell asleep to his quiet singing, lullabies I had long forgotten.

The next morning I woke slowly and painfully. I did not try to move for a long time. I lay still, gazing at the patterns of silvery light shining across the floor. My mind was calm for the first time in many days. All was silent in my ruinous attic—no sounds of life from below, no voices to comfort. Even the streets outside made few interruptions. Maybe it was still early? Maybe it was Sunday? The whole world moves slowly on Sunday mornings. I didn't know, or care.

I was hungry, but I had run out of food. I needed to go out and find something to eat. My stomach moved and growled, but I was so very tired, and my foot throbbed, and I knew that if I waited long enough, the hunger would turn to pain, and the pain to a dull emptiness that would not seem so bad. I lay still, until I slept again.

Waking, again. I could tell by the light that much of the day had passed. I would have to move eventually, and it was better to do it while there was still light. I got up slowly, first rolling onto my side, then up onto my knees. I crawled first—I would have to crawl to a wall or post so I could pull myself up. Broken glass crunched beneath my knees, scraping and grinding. I reached the nearest windowsill and pulled myself up, putting weight at first only on my good leg. Tenderly, I tried to step onto my right foot, just a little. It seemed okay, so I tested it a little more. Pounding pain came in waves—much worse than last night—and then I felt an awful cracking in my foot, something snapping.

I gave up. I would stay in the attic.

Above all, the child's captivity must remain a secret.

Night. Cold. I put on all my clothes, except for my extra underwear. I burrowed into my sleeping bag and covered up my head, and when it became difficult to breathe I made a sort of air shaft.

When I next woke to daylight, I felt even worse. But it seemed like I had slept longer. Maybe I could just sleep the time away until my birthday. Maybe I could just not wake up. I was so tired and weary that it didn't seem to matter anymore.

But then I realized that my mouth was a desert, and I remembered that I hadn't been to the bathroom since the storm. *I must be really dehydrated*, I thought. *I need to get some water.* So, I began to crawl again, and then I kind of hopped and limped over to the attic door, making a lot of noise on the way. That reckless feeling returned, and I didn't even try to be quiet.

I stopped to rest a moment at the door, knowing that I had two flights of stairs ahead of me, and as my breathing slowed, I heard a noise on the other side of the door. Floorboards creaking. Someone was coming up the stairs. I had nowhere to hide, and not enough time anyway. I waited, and as the door opened I took a deep breath.

It was her, the gentle woman with the strawberry blond hair. She was wearing normal clothes, jeans and a flowing white shirt, but I was certain she was the woman from my daydream, from Alateen. And she was real; she was not like my dad and the physicists.

"I'm sorry."

I whispered, because I could not find my voice. I looked at her, and I felt my father standing behind me, and his presence made me feel safe, and suddenly I did not want to leave my attic. I wanted to stay there, with him.

But I knew that I could not. And, somehow, I wasn't scared anymore. The dream-woman looked at me without saying anything at first; she saw my swollen foot and how I was leaning against the wall. In that moment, that very, very small grain of time, she knew who I was, and why I was there.

I stepped toward her on my good foot, and hopped through the threshold, leaving my father behind.

"It's okay, sweetie," she said. "It's going to be okay." And she put her arms around me, and they were strong arms, just like in my dream.

Her name was Gwen, and she told me that she and some of the others had been hearing noises in the attic for some time. They had suspected that someone was squatting there, but it was really not unusual to find the occasional squatter in the attic. Still, they eventually began to worry. They wanted to send one of the guys up with Gwen, just in case, but she didn't want to frighten whoever was up there. Now she needed help getting me down the stairs, and she called down to someone I could not see. The footsteps were heavy; it was a man, and as I watched him step from the shadows around the stairway landing, I was seized with fear. A man in a dark jacket, wearing a trilby.

I screamed.

I didn't even try to restrain myself. My own voice, usually stifled, buried somewhere deep inside my chest, frightened me.

Gwen held my hand tightly. "Honey, it's okay. It's just Robert. He's a friend. He's going to help carry you down the stairs. Is that okay?"

I looked at Gwen's face only, refusing to turn my head toward the man on the stairs. She was telling the truth.

"Okay," I whispered.

He stepped more lightly, walked more slowly, and I summoned up the courage to look at him, and he was harmless, just an artsy guy, tall and lanky, wearing a trilby that he pulled off much better than my stepfather did. And his jacket was not black, but pale blue. He seemed all right, but I still cringed when he picked me up. When my feet left the ground, I felt the fear again, and I wanted to jump back onto the floor, even though I knew the pain it would cause. But I let him carry me to Gwen's loft, a big open room with dried flowers and sweet smelling candles and transparent curtains that billowed in the evening breeze. I felt safe there. I spilled my story before she could even ask, while she helped me to her sofa and washed my foot with warm cloths and then bandaged it.

"You know, I'll have to take you to the hospital," she said slowly. I looked up into her big blue eyes, and I saw my mother, before—before all of our tragedy. I trusted her.

"Yes, I know." Somehow, I knew that Gwen would protect me. I knew I would not be going back to the terrible house. And maybe things would be okay. Maybe I could still see my mom and my baby sister again.

First, she brought me soup, and lots of water, and she let me sleep for a little while. On Gwen's couch, I slept more deeply and peacefully than I had in a very long time, maybe years, and I was sorry to awake.

"Matilda," Gwen woke me gently, rubbing my shoulder. "We should go to the hospital before it gets too late."

I stirred, waking slowly. I felt like a sick child, safe in my mother's care. The daylight was waning; orange and pink light painted the sky in the west windows behind Gwen, and I realized that she looked a little less like the woman in my daydream. But she was capable, I could tell. She did not have lost eyes, like my mom and April and April's friend and probably me.

After a few more minutes, Gwen left to find Robert again so he could help me to the car. She left her door open, and I heard them approaching. Their words echoed in the hallway outside.

"I know you want to help, but she's a minor," he was saying. "I think we have to tell someone."

Gwen must have been speaking more softly, because I could not hear her reply.

"Someone is probably looking for her," I heard Robert say.

Oh, yes. Someone was looking for me.

Gwen shushed him, and they returned, and Robert carried me down the stairs and across the street to Gwen's car and lifted me carefully into the passenger's side.

"We don't have to worry about anything except for your foot tonight," she said. "And then we'll come home and rest, and in the morning, everything will be okay."

What reason did I have to trust her? And what about Robert? I knew Gwen was not really the woman from my dream, and I doubted that anyone could protect me. But I was so very tired of everything, and it had been such a long time since someone had told me that everything would be okay.

I decided to believe her. I stared out the side window as Gwen started the car and began to drive, and I watched the factory recede and disappear behind us. My chest felt just a little lighter, and when I looked down at my hands, they were no longer trembling.

Matthew Hance

Matthew Hance is happily married with a kickass four-year-old son, and even though he lives in Columbus, Ohio, he's a diehard Nittany Lions fan.

When he's not busy working for the State, he's either surfing the net, posing his action figures or in a video-game-induced coma.

Matt's first published short story, "Uncurable," was included in the award winning anthology *Twisted Tails*. His novel-in-progress, *CML*, made it to the finalist round in TheNextBigWriter.com's 2010 Strongest Start competition.

THE GRANDEST TRICK

By Matthew Hance

There are three imperative rules a magician must always follow. Number one: always protect your secrets. Number two: always stay one step ahead of the person you're trying to fool. And number three: everything that happens must add to the final illusion.

For example, sitting in the second row, there is a lovely woman wearing a trimming blue-floral dress. A poodle haircut outlines her smile as I take a nickel she offers and clap it swiftly between my gloved hands. I open them just as fast to reveal a long-stemmed rose. With one hand, I toss the rose to my beautiful patron. With the other, I slip her coin into my jacket pocket.

I receive a round of mild applause from the audience. Except one man. He glares at me with his arms crossed—right through a pair of tortoise-shell sunglasses. I pay him no attention, for I already predicted his arrival.

"Thank you," I say as the applause fades. "Thank you very much. You're all too kind."

I'm back onstage waltzing around, looking curiously at some curtain-covered objects. There's the ghost house. The guillotine. I run my fingers over the arc of the spinning wheel, pretending I'm pondering which trick to perform next. But I already know. It's all part of the greater plan.

An overwhelming shriek takes the room by surprise. I swing around in shock, scanning the crowd with my hand shading my eyes from the glaring light in the ceiling. Fifty-some faces all point me in the direction of Miss Floral Dress standing on top of her chair, grasping the backrest for dear life. She's staring at the floor, hyperventilating.

"Ma'am," I say, stepping down into the aisle. "Is everything okay?"

She rattles the chair like a maraca and almost tips over in the process. "I'm far from okay! Your rose turned into that hideous thing down there!"

She shoots it a terrified glance, and the crowd follows, huddling around in a circle to see what all the fuss is about. Once someone announces, "It's a snake!" the circle expands. Everyone except that mysterious stranger—he remains seated, keeping his gaze locked on me.

The crowd turns to me for an answer, so I raise my hands to hush them, saying, "Remain calm, people. I don't know where the snake came from, but I'll handle it. Just don't make any sudden moves,"—which really translates into, *Don't leave just yet.*

A few children are burrowed in their parent's arms. The woman is shivering. And someone is slipping a knife from a pocket, so I point to a man poking his head out from behind the woman and shout, "You, sir!"

He bobs a thumb at himself.

"Yes, you. Would you be so kind as to wrangle the snake and bring it to the stage?"

He scrunches his face into wrinkles and mumbles something incomprehensible.

"Very well."

I pull a fist-sized balloon out of my jacket pocket and let it rise so everyone can see. I yank the string several times, causing something inside the green sphere to rattle. And before anyone can question what's going on, I bring the balloon to my lips and blow it toward the man. Once it's rising over his head, I snap my fingers and it pops, dropping the woman's coin onto his head. I say, "If you will not help this poor woman out of the pure generosity of your heart, what say you to accepting her money?"

I start to see people breathing a bit easier. Some are even cracking a smile. Others are *Ooh-ing* and *Ah-ing*. The stranger isn't fazed.

My hired help digs the coin out of his hair, slips it in his pants pocket and kneels down to confront the hissing snake which is coiled like a loaded spring.

As he goes at it with one shaking hand, I say, "Use two hands, good man. This isn't your snake we're dealing with here."

Ladies blush. Men chuckle. Children ask, "What's so funny?"

And he dashes at the creature like a master, snatching it up in one swift motion. Just like grabbing hold of an out-of-control garden hose—a move only professionals can make.

"Very close," I say, looking at another woman next to him, shying away from him and his new friend. "Your name, ma'am?"

She fakes a smile. "Ruth."

I look at the hero. "And shall I call you Mr. Snake Catcher?"

"Call me Joe."

"Okay, Joe." I motion toward the stage. "Why don't we stand up there so the snake doesn't bite poor Ruth?"

"Up there?"

"Yes. Now on with you!"

I give him a pat and we're off. Once in position, I take

his hands and re-clamp them around the snake's neck. "Hold tight, you hear? One bite from this undersized snake has enough venom to kill three men, so any gaffe could be deadly."

He nods as he secretly pokes a piece of dead snake, which is pre-looped, out through his hands.

I say, "Ladies and gentlemen, this foul beast has intruded on the show. Was it welcome?"

Someone shouts, "No!"

"Exactly, because it did not pay for a ticket."

I get a few laughs, but they end when I raise my right hand, holding a rusty pair of open scissors. The snake's loop wiggles, thanks to Joe's thumbs, as the V-shaped blades slice into its skin. "Now it will pay the ultimate price!" I squeeze the handles and dig in the blades. Blood runs down the sides and guts ooze out.

I yell, "Death!" and finish the cut. Then I take hold of one of the severed chunks and toss it into the crowd.

Just as expected, everyone is appalled. They're a symphony of gasps. I even evoke a reaction from the stranger. He's reaching into his brown, woolen suit. I catch the butt of a gun against the backdrop of his orange shirt before swatting Joe's hands away to reveal an unharmed, fidgeting snake. It even hisses for good measure as I raise it into the spotlight.

Almost instantly, it hits the crowd, and they put their hands together for the raucous applause I was looking for. Some even whistle and holler. The stranger withdraws his hand and lets his suit jacket fall over the gun.

"Thank you," I say, taking a bow. "You're all great sports, really." I do a few dips. "Too kind. Too kind." Then I take the snake and smush it between my hands. When I flip them open, another rose is left behind. I toss it to Ruth and say,

"Don't worry, dear, I promise that one won't go rotten."

She hesitantly takes the flower.

"Just remember, people," I say in a louder voice, "this is merely a taste of what awaits tomorrow night for the special Halloween show. Be sure to tell your friends and family!"

As people start to file out, I hear them talking amongst each other, tossing positive adjectives around with my stage name. A good performance, indeed.

I hold a mighty smile even though that stranger is out of his seat and walking in my direction.

"You'd like an autograph?" I ask, staring not at him, but the remaining people flooding out into the street.

"Not exactly," he says, digging around in his pants pocket. "Clever show you got yourself."

"I try."

He smiles at me as he rummages. "I bet you do. Couldn't tell what was an act and what wasn't. Until the end, of course."

"Mister…"

"Gamble. Call me Gamble."

"Very well, Gamble. What can I do for you?"

He finally plucks out a gold badge and holds it right up to my face. Lint is caught on the sharp edges. The engraved name reads Detective Gamble. He lets his sunglasses fall down his nose so we can make eye contact. "Looking for a boy named Pauly Dean," he says. "Went missing a few days ago." He squints real hard and then glares the same way. "Most likely from here."

I gently slide my glove off and start to nibble on my thumbnail. If this isn't obvious enough, I don't know what is. I take a big gulp when I ask, "Here, meaning?"

"This little carnival."

He pushes the sunglasses back up his nose, crams the badge into his pocket and starts to climb the stage stairs. One by one, his shoes pounding the planks sound awfully like, *Caught. You. Pedophile.* He says, "Boy lives a half mile away. Mom says he always wanders off down here. Spends hours on end but always comes home at night. This time he didn't. Mom hasn't heard from him since."

"That's terrible," I say, following him up the stairs. "What's the dad think?"

"Not sure. I'll find out when he's sober." He points at the stage door. "What's in there?"

With one quick loop, I'm in between him and the door, assaulted by cinnamon cologne and lavender detergent—a deadly combination of odors. "A trick," I say with a cough.

"A trick?"

"My grandest trick."

He tries to peek over my shoulder, but I shift. "Why do you need three huge padlocks? Seems more like a secret, doesn't it?"

"It is a secret. All tricks are secret. If you deciphered them, there'd be no magic left. Only dexterous trickery."

He cracks a smile, blowing cool mint in my face. Man of many smells meets the man of many secrets.

"Please," I say, motioning away from the stage. "I need to prepare for tomorrow."

Gamble takes his jacket and peels it over the silver gun.

"Detective, I've already seen that."

"Then I don't think you get the point. I'm looking for a lost child. Bowl-cut blonde hair, an inch long. Light skin. Last wearing blue jeans and a long-sleeved shirt. Red." With his other hand he pulls a picture out of his pants pocket and shoves it in my face. I hear his voice from behind a close-up of Pauly's smile. "Have you seen him?"

My sleeve begins to rattle—partially from my shaking arm; mostly from the wriggling snake. A hiss funnels out and Gamble drops the picture, takes a step back. "What was that?"

I lower my arm and the snake slides out. I grab it by the head and lift it up. "Squirmy thing—trying to get away."

Gamble takes another step back. "You let a poisonous snake hide in your sleeve?"

"Not really." I flick the creature's head, prompting it to cock its jaw. I point at the teeth and say, "It's de-venomed. I would never put my audience in danger."

Even through the wall of sunglasses I can see his eyes roll.

"Whatever," he says. He rests one hand on the gun's handle and stabs a finger at the door with the other. "I'd like to see what's in there."

I smile deviously. "I don't think so, Detective. You see, I have rights, and you have no cause. I would never harm a child, and until you find evidence to prove otherwise, please, like I said before, be on your way."

He sighs, staring at his foot tapping away on the floorboards. He's clearly distraught but trying to play his hand wisely. People only get so many cards and it's a shame to lose one.

"Okay," he mumbles. "I'll play along." He stares right at me so I can see myself in the reflection of his glasses. "Let's say I'll come by tomorrow night for your big show. Maybe you'll change your tune then."

I look into my own eyes and say, "As long as you pay for

a ticket, be my guest."

He finally lets the jacket fall down to his side before turning and walking away—thinking he got the needed information. The only problem is, he's neglecting rule number three.

***

Dimple-faced Pauly was an eager explorer. Young and sly, he slipped in through the front entrance—a squeaky wooden door with faulty hinges—thinking his arrival had gone unnoticed. It had for a moment, as I was onstage marveling over a handmade, oak guillotine. But I sensed his movements as he tiptoed down the aisle.

His feet dragged on the carpet. His knees bumped chairs. And he breathed heavily. Bad traits for a sneak.

Then, nothing. I swung around to find Pauly plopped down in a seat with his smiling face resting on the chair in front of him. A blonde bowl cut. Red shirt. Jeans. And his eyes— one of which swollen green, outlined in black and blue—held a look of excitement and adventure.

"Why, hello," I said, tipping my top hat to him. "You're a bit early today."

He nodded.

"Very well," I said, clapping my hands together. "So, would you like to see my latest secret?"

And just like that, Pauly hopped out of his seat and ran up onstage. He seemed ready. Like he was where he belonged.

"This just arrived today," I said, running my hand along the wood of a six-by-three foot rectangular box. I gave the side a knock; it echoed inside. "Hollow."

He followed suit—his tiny knock's echo diminishing much faster than mine had.

My hand stopped at one of the two masts, and I ran a finger inside a long groove extending to the top. "This is the path the mouton follows." His eyes darted up to the steel blade. The razor-sharp edge sparkled in the light. He didn't say anything, but if he'd said one word, I knew it would've been, "Unreal!"

I looped around to the front and pointed at the lunette. "Now this is where I'll have a hired audience member come up, lay belly-down and fit their head through. Go ahead. Feel it."

As his curious fingers felt around the neck hole, I snuck the dangling rope into my hand. With one tug, the blade plummeted. But a steel plate hidden above the hole halted its fall. Pauly didn't move his hand an inch—a strange reaction for a child.

At that point, I heard the faint yell of a woman. She sounded frantic.

I placed my hand atop his and pushed down, revealing that the board below the neck hole was really made of rubber and split down the center.

"When the blade falls, my hired help will push his head through the rubber and drop his upper body down into the box below. A dull blade that's been resting on his neck the entire time will fill the hole and look like an actual blade, thus convincing people that I have decapitated an audience member."

And finally, he said, "Whoa."

The woman's yelling became louder, as if she were running laps up and down the dirt street.

"Son," I said to Pauly, my tone rushed. "I think your time has come."

I quickly led him over to the back door. "I had something in store for the Halloween show, but now I've changed my mind." I flung open the door and said, "Look at this—I've prepared a room, specially for you. Beats your couch at home, doesn't it?"

He nodded and I nudged him inside.

***

"Halloween!" I announce, lifting my silken black cape in each hand to resemble stretched wings. Overhead bulbs hanging from the ceiling are my stage lighting. They also set the eerie mood for the nearly one hundred audience members. "'Tis a time of celebration and superstition." Using my right hand, I fan the cape over my face, revealing a plastic devil mask with bull horns, angry eyes and a cocked-open bear-trap mouth. "Boo!"

I get a few gasps. One shriek. A couple of laughs. And one detective staring at me behind a wall of sunglasses.

"Halloween has long been thought of as the day when the dead return to the earth." With my left hand, I fan the cape over the devil mask, turning it into a hollowed-out skull with craters for eyes. A few people clap. Some children cower away. Mr. Gamble waits patiently to make his move.

"The ancient Celts lit bonfires!" I snap my fingers, and a metal bowl on a table behind me sparks a flame inside, turning a lump of barley into a small fire. "And they wore costumes to ward off the roaming ghosts!" In one motion, I pull off my cape, showing the crowd my costume—a white-and-black-barred jumpsuit with a puffy clown mask concealing my head.

I leap off the stage and rush up to a boy in the first row, poking my nose into his chest. "Go ahead. Give it a honk."

He looks to his father who nods, then hooks his small finger and thumb into a "C" around the red ball on my nose. He squeezes, producing a "boink" sound.

I walk backward up the stage stairs, saying, "Take a look in your pocket, young man."

He pats himself and finds a lump in his jacket. He immediately sticks his hand inside and withdraws a paper bag stuffed with taffy, gummy bears, bubblegum and licorice. "Sweet!" he yelps, and I respond, "Literally."

That was just a little filler. You can't just go from big trick to big trick. There has to be a buildup. Especially after taking a real audience member, shackling him to the spinning board and throwing knives at him. The man's body was outlined with a dozen blades, yet none had harmed a hair on him. I even had him hold a balloon sideways with his mouth so I could use the last knife to pop it. The crowd went bonkers. I wonder what they'll think of my grandest trick.

"Ladies and gentlemen!" I holler, fanning my arms outward. The fire extinguishes and the overhead bulbs transform into shrinking white dots that disappear with a flash in the darkness.

It's silent. Dead silent. I hold for a moment. There are whispers. *Hold a bit longer.*

Then, there are questions. "What's going on?" and "What's going to happen?"

It's time.

"Behold!" I shout. The bulbs flicker back on to reveal me standing next to the ten-foot-tall guillotine. My clown mask, and all the others, are crammed neatly in my sleeves.

I give the crowd a moment to refocus before outlining the towering masts with my hands. It's very important to be

95

articulate. Posture and gestures are key. And drama. It's necessary to be overly dramatic.

"A barbaric method of execution that dates all the way back to the mid-1500s!" I place my boot on the box and hoist myself up. With my fingers gliding over the blade, I continue, "They say the person guillotined becomes unconscious very quickly and dies from shock and anoxia due to hemorrhage— all in less than 60 seconds. It has often been reported that the eyes and mouths of people beheaded have shown signs of movement." I stare at one of the children in the first row as I say, "Imagine having a conversation with a severed head."

I sense the crowd is on edge. They're bringing my words to life with their imaginations—becoming fearful of the device, exactly as they're supposed to. It makes it all that much easier when I say, "Don't be frightened, my lovely people! Besides, I need a courageous volunteer to come and put their neck on the line… literally."

Nobody moves. They just look around at each other until a brave soul steps forth. But there's no need to worry, for I already found him. I point directly at Joe, sitting in the fourth row. Tonight he's wearing a silly mustache, monocle, and burlap suit.

"Sir?" I say. "Would you be willing to risk your life for this audience's enjoyment?"

Joe hesitates. He gives me looks. Unsure. Then, scared. He gives me too much time because Gamble shoots out of his seat and yells, "Over here!" Everyone looks. Everyone stares. Everyone waits. "I'll do it," he says, already in route to the aisle, banging his butt off of people's faces. "What do I have to do?"

I snicker a bit. "Sir, it's quite fine. Have a seat, please. I was talking to that man over there." I point at Joe.

But it's too late, for Gamble has cleared the stairs in one leap and is now standing before me, eagerly awaiting instructions. "Why can't I do it?" he asks.

"Umm…" I can barely see over him, and his hands—they're rubbing together as if to create fire. I halt his fire-starting with an enclosing fist, lean in and whisper, "So you did come to play."

"Seems I did."

"Very well, listen carefully. You'll lie on the table belly-down and then I'll strap you in. When I tell the crowd that 'people in the front row might get a bit wet,' that's your cue to start counting down silently from ten. On two, I'll release the rope and drop the blade. On one, you'll push your head down through the rubber neckpiece into the box below, making it appear as though you've lost your head."

He gives me a pat on the back and says, "Sure, sure. You helped me. Now let me help you." He goes over and hops up on the table. After cracking all of his knuckles, he flips over and slides his head through the neck hole, chuckling a bit after spotting the secret entrance.

As I'm sealing the top part of the lunette, I say, in a raised voice, "This is extremely dangerous, so I must warn the audience to never stick your head inside a guillotine. That is, unless you want to lose it."

I shackle Gamble's wrists and ankles to the box with curved, metal bars. "And if I slip up here tonight… well, that will only reaffirm that you must not play around with execution devices."

I get a few laughs, but for the most part, it's obvious that people are nervous. Even more so when I take the tattered rope in my hand and say, "People in the front row might get a bit wet."

My mental countdown begins. Ten. Nine. Eight.

POW! What sounds like a muffled shot erupts in the distance.

And darkness! The bulbs once again flash off. "What's going on?" Gamble asks, wiggling around in the deathtrap. "What was that noise?"

"Remain calm," I say. "People, remain calm. It seems we're experiencing technical difficulties."

Everyone was calm until then. Now, there's lots of shifting and whispering.

Three. Two. One. The lights flash back on. The crowd leans in. Gamble stretches out his neck to see what happened.

"You still have your head," I say, "for it seems the spirits have spared your life." I walk around the stage for a few moments before unshackling the good detective. Then I bob a thumb to the top of the rope where it's tied into seven bulky knots.

Gamble is on his feet, patting himself down, and even takes off his sunglasses. I merely smile, placing a hand on the four-foot-tall object draped by a black curtain on my left.

"Perhaps we'll find the answers we seek," I pull off the cloth to reveal a gutted doll house with a large roof sitting alone on a fold-out table. "Here, in the ghost house."

The crowd leans in closer.

"Dear, sir," I say to the detective, "will you please scan the house to make sure it's empty?"

Poor Gamble is giving me the curious eye as he hesitantly sticks his arm through the two-by-two foot home. When he's done, I rotate the fold-out table so everyone can see.

Then I take a single rocking chair out of my pocket, place it on the floor and shut both sets of doors.

"Spirit," I say, closing my eyes, acting as if I'm calling upon all of my energy, "show yourself!"

I ease open the doors, and in the rocking chair sits a plain white doll with no face. The crowd gasps. Gamble is trying to figure out how I did it, but I close the doors once again and say, "Spirit, that is not your true form. Please, show yourself!"

Again, I ease the doors open, this time revealing a much bigger doll that barely fits inside. Its body is bent in half, and the rocking chair is in pieces on the floor.

Everyone's amazed, but the trick isn't over. There's one more part.

After closing the doors for a third time, I say, "Spirit, please right the wrong you have done and return that which you have stolen from my poor volunteer!"

I feel Gamble's eyes burning a hole in me as I swing the doors open. There, on the floor, is his gun. He immediately slips a hand inside his jacket and feels the empty holster.

"Go ahead." I step out of the way. "The spirits have returned your firearm, Detective."

He's infuriated as he swipes up the gun and notices a piece of paper attached to the trigger. It reads, "Your move," and I guess it doesn't help that the crowd is going nuts, giving me a thunderous round of applause.

Gamble's aimless stare tells the whole story. He's looking right through me for an answer that doesn't exist. *How was I fooled?* he's thinking. *Those laughs are meant for me.* He'll always wonder, *What's the secret to that trick?*

I see his emotions climax as he crumbles the note and bobs his gun. His ego is deflated, his wits bested. As he slowly aims the shaking gun at my stomach, I lose my grasp on certainty for the first time since his arrival.

Gamble says, "Get out," but everyone is too busy clapping, so he turns his head and screams, "Get out!" Once he waves the gun around and it sparkles in the reflection of the light, the audience begins to swarm out of the building. At the same time, a line of police officers march in. They jingle and pound all the way up the stairs, stopping right in front of the padlocked door.

Then Gamble regains his confidence. He gushes with excitement as he pulls his own surprise out of his pocket and forces it in my face—a search warrant.

"I was already one step ahead of you," he says, nudging me in the side with the gun. "Now if you would be so kind as to unlock that door, we can all get on with our nights rather quickly. Except you, of course."

"But I have plans for tonight, Detective."

"Open." He places the cold tip of the gun on my Adam's apple. "Now."

I stumble over to the charcoal-colored door, two police officers standing on either side, and say, "No."

"Fine." He smiles, gesturing to his men. "Have it…"

"Don't bother with that," I say, taking the padlocks and flipping them off to reveal nothing but an unlocked door. "It's merely an illusion."

The officers ping-pong confusion back and forth. It slaps Gamble in the face. I want to say, "Your move," but I don't have to. He raises his gun and commands, "Open it." And just like the ghost house, when I open the door, there's nothing inside but a gutted room.

"This is my storage area," I say. "Everything I have is

currently onstage."

Gamble storms inside—his anger echoing off of the walls right back at him. He pouts. Kicks the floor. Shrugs. Curses. Mumbles. Sighs. When he sees me smiling, he shouts, "Get him out of my face!"

Two officers pin my hands behind my back before falling silent. As Gamble stands there tapping his foot, one of them says, "Where to?"

Gamble takes in the emptiness for a moment. Deep breath after deep breath, I know what he's going to fill it with. He points over my shoulder and says, "Give him a seat all the way in the back. Right on the floor. Right by the entrance."

The detective thinks he's won. He gives me a wink as the two officers drag me up the aisle. They push me down and say, "Don't move." Then all the little minions swarm around their mother bee. They listen carefully as Gamble stares holes in me.

"Listen up! You see these whitewashed walls? These swept floorboards? This fancy, well-kept stage?" The minions' heads bob like the sea. "I want it all brought down! The magician doesn't think he has to reveal his secret, so we'll rip it out of him while he watches."

And indeed I watch. I watch minions kick chairs over like dominos. I watch them fill the floor with potholes. They tear cracks in my walls and gut wires like pig intestines. The longer it takes, the more patience Gamble loses. Each time he looks at me, his face is sweatier and sweatier. Powdered in dust. Muddy. Looking like a torched zombie. But then he spots some hope.

The detective takes his place onstage. He bows, and dust snows off of his hair. His pearly-white teeth are visible through his mask of black and white camouflage. He takes the opportunity to perform a little show of his own.

"Ladies and gentlemen, and way back there where you can probably barely hear me," Gamble says, flicking his hands around. "I have a very special performance planned for you tonight. Something I like to call 'Destructing the magic!'" He approaches the spinning wheel and gives it a whirl. Right as his hand withdraws, he pulls his gun out and fires at the base. Three bullets later the wheel breaks off, rolls off stage and sinks halfway into the floor.

This garners the minions' attention; when I hear someone whistle and another clap, I grind my fists into the splintered floor to release my anger. Gamble can sense this, so he slides over to the guillotine and motions to a minion who tosses him a crowbar. He shouts, "Behold!" before splitting apart one of the masts. He showcases the other mast with his outstretched hands, and everyone watches as it collapses from the pressure, ripping a hole in the box. Several strikes later, my newest trick is in pieces with Gamble's taunting face hovering overhead. I strain to hold back my emotions. Rage. The thirst for vengeance. But I can't let him see me become another object in the room.

Gamble waltzes over to the ghost house, dragging the crowbar across the stage. He gives the foldout table and gutted home a once-over before letting a laugh slip. And then he stares some more. He laughs some more. And the entire time I can see him thinking, *How'd he do it?* His eyes are saying, *Where's the secret?* He turns to a minion, but the man simply shrugs. He turns to another minion, gets more of the same. Then he finally decides to throw the crowbar at the side of the ghost house, causing it wobble on top of the table and end his performance.

But at the end of this performance, nobody claps.

Nobody whistles. Nobody cheers. As zombie officers pass by grunting and mumbling, I can't help but breathe a sigh of relief. And when the star of this disastrous show approaches, dragging his feet, carrying his jacket under his arm, I wait patiently for an autograph. I want to show him my appreciation. It's the least I can do for a man whose skin is sagging from the weight of defeat. Just as he comes within touching distance, he sticks a hand in my face, pointing a finger and says, "I know it's you."

I try to say, "There's no evidence to…" but he makes a slicing gesture at my throat with his hand and finishes with, "It's my move," before strolling off.

Once the circus is gone for good, I pounce to my feet. I'm so giddy that I skip over floor holes and leap the gap where the stage stairs once stood. I hurry over to the only intact object in the room—the ghost house. It sits onstage like a rose in the middle of a swamp. But this rose, its fragrance is victory. I take a big whiff as I unclamp the large roof and fling it open in one motion. Pauly springs out like a jack-in-the-box. His face is one big smile as he holds up his hand, waiting for me to high-five him. I do, and give the little magician's head a good rub.

"Excellent performance tonight," I say. He simply nods.

You see, the real magician isn't the person onstage taking all of the credit. The real magician is the assistant, who does all the work. One look at Pauly the first day we met and I knew he needed me—needed this adventurous life. Needed to escape his drunken father. But I also needed him. There's no magic in magic. It's all about fooling the audience, and following the rules.

Chad Jones

In the fall of 2010, Chad Jones walked away from a six-year broadcasting career with a prominent Columbus radio station, as a producer and on-air talent, to devote his energies towards writing full-time. He stands behind his decision, regardless of eating PB&J at every meal.

On most days, Chad roams the freeways of Columbus, Ohio, playing his music too loud and observing the community for new topics to write about. At night, he stays up too late on his family's ranch in Marysville, Ohio, writing and fighting for space in bed from his two best friends, Boris and Tank—a bullmastiff and English mastiff.

Chad is also an editor and contributor for the 2011 edition of Columbus State's annual literary arts magazine, *Spring Street*.

Chad enjoys reading and responding to all of his email, please contact him at ProducerChadJones@yahoo.com.

This work proudly presented by the following sponsor

Gretel's Handcrafted Soap

Gretel's soap is handmade with all-natural ingredients in Columbus, Ohio.

www.GretelsHandcraftedSoap.com

THE ROAD AHEAD

By Chad Jones

Emily sprinted toward the mailbox at the end of the driveway. Her cell phone, tucked snuggly in the back pocket of her favorite skinny jeans, stridently poured the soundtrack to her resentment for this town through the headphones.

But she didn't hear the music. She heard the future applause of the crowd as she walked across the stage to grab her high school diploma. She heard the drama of her pregnant best friend, Ally, disappear. And she heard the conversation last Christmas with her grandpa replay in her mind with each ambitious stride.

***

"How did Grandma react when you told her you were a poet?" Emily asked.

Grandpa Joe chuckled and took a deep breath.

"The way every other woman did. She thought it was romantic... until she read a few of my poems."

"Whadya mean?" Emily asked, thumbing through a collection of his poems.

"Well," he paused and took a sip of his tea. "Most women get all mushy when a guy says he writes poetry. But that's because most guys write poetry *to get* women." Joe set his cup down and leaned back in the chair. "My poems weren't what women wanted to hear."

Emily lifted her eyes from the book and scrunched her face, showing further confusion.

"I didn't write about love, peace or war like every other poet in the sixties. I wrote about life," Joe said.

"But wasn't that what life was all about back then?"

Joe chuckled again. "You've been listening to the Beatles too much."

Emily rolled her eyes and went back to reading the book.

"There's something very beautiful about taking ordinary, everyday objects and painting them in a light that most people never see. That's how I wrote."

"You mean like the poem about the bathtub? The one about loneliness?"

"Exactly, pumpkin. And, you know, I see the same kinda style in many of your poems. You've made some serious progress in the last year."

"Really? I've just been writing more and reading some of the poets you told me to study," Emily replied.

Joe leaned forward and rested his hand on her knee. "Emily, you truly have a gift. You just keep doing what you're doing. You'll get there."

She sat the book in her lap and put both of her hands on his.

Her voice rose with excitement. "I SO wish I could be here in San Francisco with you! Just think about how much better I would get then!"

Joe looked in her eyes and calmly lowered his voice. "Remember, it's not about *where* you see the world. It's about *how* you see it."

"I know, but this is where all the best writers and artists came from."

He leaned back again in his chair. "Listen. Haight-Ashbury isn't what it used to be, sweetie. At one point, we could have changed the world with our art." Joe took a deep breath and stroked his grey beard. "But now it seems like most of the good ones traded their notepads in for a 401K."

Emily watched the disappointment tumble down his face.

"After all these years, I still wonder what might have been. We were *supposed* to make the world better for our children and grandchildren."

Emily picked up the teapot and topped off his cup. "You know, Grandpa, you still can."

Joe lifted his cup. He held it under his lips for a moment and sat it back down on the table. "Maybe you're right." He cracked a smile. "I'll tell you what."

Emily's eyes opened wide with curiosity as she sipped from her cup.

"You graduate high school, and I'll not only let you come stay and study with me, I'll give you a thousand bucks to fly out here."

Emily's cup slipped from her grip and smashed on the hardwood floor. "Oh my gosh! I'm so sorry, Grandpa!"

Joe laughed lightly and got up from his chair. He walked over to the side of Emily's chair, knelt down, and started picking up the broken shards.

"Just promise me you won't go breaking all my good teacups when you get out here."

Her face lit up with a smile.

***

She stopped running, her Chuck Taylors sliding across the dirt.

Barely eighteen and eagerly planning her escape from this Midwestern town—where drinking beer and having babies was the main form of entertainment—Emily prayed that what she so desperately wanted was waiting for her inside that mailbox.

"Oh *come on*, Grandpa!" she impatiently slid in between her heavy breaths. "How long are you gonna wait to send me the *damn* check?!"

She knew her grandfather didn't have much money. She also knew he wouldn't let her down. He never did. But with only days until her graduation ceremony, she was growing anxious.

Emily stood on the road, continuing to breathe heavily. Slamming the mailbox shut and turning to head back down her driveway, she grabbed the cell phone from her back pocket and changed the song to the Beatles. She turned up the volume, smiled, and thought of Grandpa Joe.

Barreling down the vacant road, a driver swerved off the road, kicking up dust and gravel. As Emily lifted her eyes off the screen, her dreams of heading west disintegrated.

With one hand on a can of beer and the other reaching for a pack of cigarettes in the glove box, the driver of the dirty-black pickup truck collided with Emily's body. The bones in her legs snapped like dry spaghetti noodles, throwing her frail, petite frame in the air, smashing her face violently into the hood—her body finally rolling down onto the hot black concrete.

The truck came to a screeching halt.

"JESUS-FUCKING-CHRIST!" Tommy screamed.

He hurtled out of his truck, clumsily tripping over his boots and stumbling to find his balance. "WHY WERE YOU STANDING IN THE MIDDLE OF THE GOD-DAMN ROAD?!"

Hair covered her face, hiding any signs of life. Tommy raced over, hoping she wasn't injured worse than the impact seemed. His hope dimmed the closer he came. He bumbled to a stop, thinking of something helpful to say. His bloodshot eyes widened as he watched her blood starting to pool on the pavement.

"Are... you okay?" his voiced rumbled with fear.

She didn't respond. His words were useless.

He bent down and stretched out his hand inches from her mouth, feeling for her breath. Nothing.

Tommy quickly glanced to his right, then to his left, looking for anyone who had witnessed the accident. Nobody.

Her house sat directly off the road to the right. It looked empty. There were no other houses in either direction for several miles, only rows and rows of cornfields. Tommy knew locals didn't travel this old country road much, especially during the early afternoon. He had known that even before he skipped off the job site early that day.

Her cell phone, jarred loose during the impact, lay a few feet from her body. It still blared the music that, moments before, had flowed through Emily's soul.

Tommy picked it up. Gleaming at him through the crack in the screen, a picture of an old man standing on the Golden Gate Bridge and giving a peace sign was set as the background.

He took a couple of deep breaths and contemplated whom he could call.

9-1-1 meant police.

He had been drinking. No.

If he called anyone at work, they would know he left early and surely fire him.

Again. No.

He didn't have any real friends or family he could rely on. Solitude was his closet companion, and that wasn't much help now.

He quickly tossed the phone in the truck, ripping the headphones from the jack to stop the flow of music.

He had to think fast.

He thought about his father, how he had abandoned Tommy as a baby. What would *he* do? He thought about his mother and wondered if, through her bipolar disorder, she would know what to do.

Then the night he choked his ex-wife when she wouldn't let him see his son; the three long years he spent locked up for aggravated assault. He thought of the judge and her conditions for his parole, and how he promised himself he would never go back to prison, no matter what.

He thought about the cornfields. And the shovel in the bed of his truck.

With the ignition still running, Tommy snapped into action and walked around to the rear of the vehicle. He grabbed the shovel and chucked the rusty spade near the girl's body. As he swung back around the driver's side to park the truck in the ditch where it wouldn't be seen from the road, her phone vibrated.

She had an incoming text message, the word Mom heading the note.

theres a lettr from ur g-pa in the kitchen. ur dad n i wont b home til l8tr scrolled across the screen.

Tommy climbed behind the steering wheel, placed a cigarette between his lips and pulled another lukewarm beer from the case on the seat. With his right arm stretched out, shifting the clutch into reverse, the inside of his forearm revealed a poorly inked prison tattoo.

Scribbled in Old English letters, it read, "Trust Is Earned."

Tommy cracked open the beer and lit the cigarette. He had work to do.

Brad Pauquette

Brad Pauquette lives in Woodland Park, a neighborhood on Columbus's near east side, with his wife, Melissa, and son, Theodore. He works as an independent web developer, specializing in website and graphic design for small businesses and micro-entrepreneurs (BradPauquetteDesign.com).

Brad's first piece, "Determinism," is a science fiction foray into the origins of the universe that he hopes you won't take too seriously. The second, "Appraisal," is a dark comedy that he also hopes you won't take too seriously.

Brad and Melissa also run a grassroots, non-profit organization – The Water Cycle Project. The initiative raises money to drill fresh water bore wells in rural India, primarily by organizing long distance bicycling trips within the state of Ohio.

Please visit WaterCycleProject.org for more information about the organization, or to join Brad on a cycling tour.

This work proudly presented by the following sponsor

WaterCycleProject.org

The Water Cycle Project

Well, water you waiting for?

www.WaterCycleProject.org

DETERMINISM
By Brad Pauquette

The old man was playing with his balls again when Hudson came in.

"You are exactly predictable," Stanley said as Hudson closed the heavy front door of the century-old home behind him. "I would fix the ringer, but you are the only one who comes, and always at one of two precise moments in the day."

Eight years ago Hudson had helped him move the billiards table in.

"I enjoy a game of which precision is the object," Dr. Stanley Hopewell had told him as they heaved the 700 pound slate table up the front steps, grating the heirloom quality wood against the cement. Stanley always had a way of talking like that. A manner which was technically superior, or "precise" as he would have claimed, but really only convoluted the message and made one pause, suspicion or stupidity burned in the eyes, before a commensurate response could be mounted.

Though he had stopped in at least once a week for the better part of a decade, Hudson didn't know what exactly Stanley was a doctor of, and it wouldn't have surprised him if the answer was nothing. Stanley claimed to have invented the modern polygraph machine in 1944, a year before John E. Reid. By his own admission he was only 12 years old at the time.

The doctor claimed that his young psyche rejected reality and he was hospitalized when he could find no truthful human being to use as a control for testing his machine. His parents parted out his gadgets to pay the mounting price of his adolescent care.

Nonetheless, the "doctor" held the patents and credit for

a variety of items we use every day. Apparently coming to terms with the mendacity of man, he most notably invented the credit card in 1949 and developed a chemical sweetener for the first diet soda in 1951.

For the past eight years the old man had spent his days rolling the ceramic balls up and down the green felt, or so Hudson thought, and he wondered if that psychiatrist nearly seven decades earlier had done such a fantastic job as everyone believed.

Seven years ago, when Hudson still would have been saddened had his septuagenarian neighbor passed on, he stopped over early one morning when the lights had been left on all night.

"I can do it every time!" the old man shouted as Hudson popped his head in the front door that cold December morning.

Stanley was hopping around the table, chicken legs sticking out from beneath his bathrobe, pot belly flopping out over the elastic waistband of his underwear. As his dignity threatened to breach the panels of his robe, he set two balls up in the middle of the field, and hopped back to the end again to roll a third ball into them to send them clattering into the far corner pockets.

"There it is again!" the old man chirped upon another success. As Hudson stepped inside, Stanley jumped up on the felt and took a slug of beer from a Styrofoam cup. "It is exactly predictable."

The old man is rather old to be up all night inventing drinking games by himself, Hudson had thought.

Hudson wished that he could have said that the old man's behavior had grown stranger over the past eight years, before that he'd been normal. But for the duration of their relationship, the old man was statically strange.

Except for this afternoon. There was an odd intrigue in

his eyes.

"I thought your wife was coming," Dr. Hopewell prodded at Hudson. It was to be a dinner engagement.

"I told you she doesn't like you," Hudson told him truthfully.

"Well I like her," Stanley said, popping into a rarely frequented melancholy tone of voice that reflected its lack of practice. "Doesn't make any sense."

"Maybe it's because you make her call you 'Doctor Hopewell.'"

"I told her several times that 'Doctor Stanley' would be just as well!" the old man retorted in earnest protest.

They both stared at the green felt, waiting for the moment to pass. Both knew it wouldn't take long. It was as if eight years ago they'd agreed that if any interaction were going to be realistic, it would require the social memory of a brain-damaged chimp.

"Do you want to go get her?" Dr. Hopewell suggested as their eyes met again.

"Should I?" Hudson asked sheepishly. "It's nice to get away from her for a few hours anyway."

Ordinarily, Hudson loved to be with his wife. But it was true, having Holly around, complete with her not-so-passive but neither-so-agressive attitude towards the old man would only further dampen whatever ordeal he was about to endure at the doctor's insistence.

"Might be longer than that," the doctor said. "Really wish you would have brought her. Probably isn't time now anyway... really wish you would have brought her."

Hudson thought Stanley sounded sincere, and he appreciated that.

He often tried, but failed, to determine why he bothered to care for the old man. Oftentimes, Hudson felt like a kid in charge of his retarded adult brother, leading him about by the hand.

He chose to believe that it was probably his boy scout's notion of caring for the elderly that prompted him to visit the old man week after week and put a stop to whatever mischief he might find.

But perhaps, Hudson also knew, it was interest as one scientist to another. In so many ways, Dr. Stanley Hopewell was the kind of scientist-engineer that every kid with a chemistry set ever wanted to be. The kind of scientist that has the freedom, and the means, to extrapolate singeing off your seventh-grade eyebrows or sending the neighbors cat into inner-orbit over a lifetime of lawless, directionless, reportless development and experimentation.

As Hudson toiled away at his corporate lab testing pharmaceuticals each day, he often wondered if he was the actual subject of the experiment. "The effects of mindless, short-sighted experiments on over-educated primates over the course of a long, unfulfilling career" would be the academic title of the study. *If there were such a study, it would certainly be the efforts of someone like Dr. Stanley Hopewell*, Hudson had chuckled to himself more than once.

There's nothing like living vicariously through a man 40 years your senior, Hudson reflected as he began to wander into the home peering at the mountain of boxes that he hadn't noticed piled in the living room.

"What are we at today?" Hudson asked the old man. "Finally getting rid of this pool table? A little progress?"

"Those are precisely opposite questions, young man."

Stanley took a moment to peer behind him at his friend kicking about the boxes he'd left littered around the living room.

"It's totally blocking your foyer, doc, and you never actually play pool, you just roll those damn balls around with
116

your hands. When can we get rid of this stupid thing?"

And before all of the words had left Hudson's mouth, he knew what the answer would be.

"As soon as you can you tell me from whence you came."

For years, that was the doctor's response. Initially, Hudson had tried to answer the question, for a time it was a sportive game. "Lunch," "my house" the answers had started, and moved on to "my mother's womb," "fate" and so forth.

Hudson didn't try to answer now, he just shook his head and found a spot on the ceiling upon which to fixate.

An odd smile graced the doctor's lips. "Perhaps tomorrow morning, my boy."

Hudson looked again at the doctor.

"There's something in the basement I want to show you," Stanley told him, motioning towards the kitchen and leading the way to the basement steps.

When Stanley had bought the house, he had the basement sunk for a laboratory. It now had 16 foot ceilings, and the descent to the cement slab floor was formidable.

Stanley hit the power to the warehouse lights that illuminated the massive area. In the middle was a large, clear plastic dome that stretched more than 20 feet in diameter and rose nearly to the ceiling.

Hudson walked directly to it as Stanley went about the basement flipping on power switches and activating his machinery.

"Is this..?" Hudson began to ask himself as he rapped on the clear material with his knuckles. "Did we test this on the pool table?"

"That's right, Hudson," the doctor chimed in without a beat. "As I told you then, and of course you remember, that is my synthesis of polyethylene that we developed right here in this basement. I bet that if we could energize that we could contain nearly anything, even fusion."

"Tupperware?" Hudson asked incredulously. "Tupperware is the answer to nuclear fusion?"

Stanley didn't respond, but instead continued to flit about the room making contact with his gizmos and machines that ran along the perimeter of the room.

While the doctor buzzed about his work around the basement lab, Hudson found the door to the dome and stepped inside. Inside all sound stopped, as if the rest of the world didn't exist. He peered out of the dome like a ceramic figure inside of a snowglobe, watching the doctor busy with his computers. He felt euphorically separated from the planet earth, as if reality were only a dream or he had invented the cosmos himself.

Huh, Tupperware, who knew? He asked himself. "Are we freezing this stuff in the dome today?" he asked aloud, but his voice didn't make it out of the enclosure.

Hudson looked around his man-size terrarium. A large computer bank sat off to one side, a grid of sixteen LCD monitors, four wide by four high, towered from the desk to the ceiling. Next to it stood an open cupboard which contained military MREs—meals that would last forever. The doctor was always certain that the end was near, and it didn't seem irregular for him to stockpile such a thing. The other half of the dome was neatly stacked with more boxes, just like the empty ones upstairs.

He walked to the boxes and read the side of one, which was labeled "Food Insurance". As he reached for the top folds to look inside, he noticed the doctor silently banging on the clear dome just a few feet away, yelling for him to come out.

"Come look at this," Stanley instructed him, beckoning for him to come to a computer monitor on the far side of the room. Hudson exited the dome and followed the doctor.

118

"Oh my gosh," Hudson blurted out like a prepubescent girl. "Is this full-spectrum imagery?"

"That's a condescending way to put it," Stanley said in seriousness. "These lenses will pick up any energy waves from the forces that form a massive planet to gamma-rays and beyond. We can see everything, all boiled down to the visible spectrum for us."

"It's truly beautiful, Stanley," Hudson admitted with an odd affection for the old man sweeping over him. "What are we looking at?"

"Each of these sixteen monitors is linked to a specially protected unit that has been rocketing out from the planet earth for four years. Of course, they're all well within the perimeter of the Milky Way still, but we've escaped the light pollution of our sun. These are distant solar systems, and you can see the galaxies beyond. Except for these three, these three are still within our solar system," he explained, indicating three of the monitors. "All sixteen of these feeds are also linked to the computer station inside of the dome."

"It's magnificent," escaped from Hudson, enraptured by the digital imagery. "You're right, I should have brought Holly."

"I'm sorry. I'm very sorry, but it's much too late for that. I really wish you would have done as I asked."

"That's okay," Hudson answered automatically without turning to see the pained, serious look in the old man's eyes.

"This is all about the pool balls," the doctor told him. He was running out of time for his coy games. "All of the conversations and experiments we've conducted over the past eight years end in this."

"I remember them all, word for word." It was true, Hudson could recall nearly any conversation he'd had in his entire life. His college choice of extra-curriculars had dampened his memory skills for a time, but the man's mind was an electromagnet for the spoken word.

Six years ago, Stanley asked Hudson over to dinner and drunkenly demonstrated a computer program he'd written. If Stanley possessed any genius, it was an ability to continuously adapt to new technology, even at such an age.

"Every action has an equal and opposite reaction," the doctor had explained to him. "Which means that every action we observe is actually a reaction to something that happened before it." He played a simulation on his computer. "If we can accurately gauge the location and speed of these pool balls at any moment in time, then we can extrapolate that in reverse and determine when an object of what mass interacted with these balls to make that happen."

"But it's not exactly the same every time, what about chaos?" Hudson had asked.

"Chaos simply insists that the same thing cannot happen twice in a row because of miniscule differences that can't be replicated. However, the differences are also reactions and are therefore predictable." The doctor gave Hudson a minute to think, though he didn't need it. "The same principle can be expanded to apply to the physical universe." Now, Hudson needed a moment.

"What about random activity?"

"Don't be naïve, there is no random activity. Things appear random only because we lack the understanding to quantify what's happening. The weather, for instance, seems chaotic and random, but it's only so because we lack the means to correctly quantify all of the variables on the planet that affect it. Weather is 100% predictable if only we could correctly identify all of the stimulae."

"But what about entropy?"

"The same answer. The universe is trending towards disorder in predictable ways. It may seem to occur randomly, but that's only because we lack reasonable methods of observing it. Subatomic and quantum laws exist. The deterioration of organic molecules to carbon may seem to occur sporadically, but if we could properly quantify the subatomic workings we would see that it is all simply a predictable response to another action, and an action before that, and so on."

Hudson took that one home with him.

Two weeks later, he asked, "what about emotional interaction, free-will?"

"Don't kid yourself," the doctor told him, again with a scotch in his hand. "We simply haven't taken the time, or the liberty with a human subject, to accurately determine the factors. Each and every reaction, emotional, verbal, moral – is simply a physical reaction to stimulae. Your body is programmed to release certain chemical and electrical responses upon various stimulae. If you find a child in distress, for instance, your brain automatically releases chemicals which cause you to help the child or turn away, there's no decision in it."

"You mean the great Dr. Stanley Hopewell believes in fate?"

"Fate is for morons and mystics, I'm talking about determinism."

Week after week the doctor continued to expound, and Hudson could find nothing to stand in the way of his logic.

Within a month, the doctor's digital camera could capture a quarter of a second of the pool table in action and trace the action back to the last time all of the balls were at rest.

"But can your program determine what acted on the first ball?" Hudson asked. "It didn't spontaneously begin to roll of its own accord."

"Good question," the doctor conceded. "A good question indeed."

For a few weeks thereafter the conversations were few.

Hudson would stop in and find the doctor a quarter-naked and half-drunk, stumbling about, up and down the basement steps in his bathrobe with a Styrofoam cup of beer. He was tinkering, and just so nothing looked dangerous, or like it might work, Hudson left him alone.

But on this fateful day at the laboratory, Hudson had the inescapable feeling, which he was drawing near to labeling guilt, that a great many tinkerings were coming together all at once.

"With these lenses we can observe enough of the universe to know the answer to the question that keeps the pool table locked in place, my boy," Stanley exclaimed to Hudson with equal parts of pride and camaraderie. "It's in place, the time has come to seal the dome."

Hudson had been lost in thought, remembering their past encounters which were all going to "end in this" as the doctor said, and as he followed Stanley to the dome like a dog on a leash he pondered these last words and hoped he hadn't missed any critical information in his daze.

Dr. Stanley Hopewell stopped at one last computer station on his way to the dome and typed a command into a very technical looking prompt. His hands shook as he jabbed the enter button with his finger.

"It's all in place now. Come, come, no time" he said, overflowing with energy.

Hudson continued to follow the doctor into the dome as instructed. But as the doctor sealed the door behind them, Hudson began to feel as if something was terribly wrong.

"No, you're not freezing us..." Hudson thought out loud as the doctor energized the polyethylene, filling a vaccuum space in the lining of the plastic dome with high-energy particles that would further isolate whatever was inside. "The plastic upstairs on the pool table... we froze the table. This doesn't make sense, it's suicide."

122

"I told you to bring Holly along," the doctor said seriously, looking into Hudson's eyes sympathetically. "But today is the day my boy! We're doing it."

The gravity of the situation came upon Hudson all at once. Five years ago, Dr. Hopewell had figured out how to deduce what had acted on the original ball. He'd put a dome over the pool table, then frozen the space inside to the temperature of 1 Kelvin with a device he'd tinkered into existence, a temperature that slows time to near annihilation. With the molecules that made up the atmosphere in the dome moving at that speed, he could accurately quantify the location and rate of every atomic particle, so he'd explained.

"Imagine trying to count the cars on a bullet train," he had coached Hudson. "Lowering the temperature slows down the atoms, and allows our sensor to pick up the mass and speed of each and every one of them."

At first it was a grainy video that the doctor said was mainly based on movement of air in the dome, but then a few months later he'd added full-spectrum digital imagery to capture the transfer of heat, sound, particles, everything.

"Every time, the balls and felt were destroyed," Hudson clambered at the doctor, as he pieced together their fate inside of the dome.

"It's too much data to capture, we have to freeze it... we have to slow it down or it won't be accurate" the doctor insisted, the confidence in his voice waning. "I'm sorry, it's the cost of progress."

"Progress for what? Everything else will be gone!" Hudson yelled at the doctor now, grabbing him by the shirt collar. "Everything else will be gone!"

"We don't know that. It will only be for a moment, then the universe will rebound and resume. If there are extra-terrestrial cultures, they may survive. Besides, we can restart," fear seized the old man's eyes and apprehension invaded his voice. Hudson shook him violently, and pulled his face close to his as if he might burn the old man with the force of rage escaping his forehead.

"Restart with what? Holly's not here! This will destroy life in the universe! Stop this now!"

"I can't stop it. We only have a split second when the 0 Kelvin blast will be in the right position to hit everything. I can't stop it once it's started. I'm sorry."

Hudson's knuckles were white around the old man's shirt, which had pulled out of his waistline.

"How long?" Hudson growled through his breath, with his eyes ablaze, stretched to reveal the entire perimeter of his iris.

"Not long. There's no timer. But about..."

Hudson threw the old man from him. Stanley's heels kicked towards the ceiling as his barrel chest receded to the floor first, his shoulder leading the way into the earth.

And in the moment between Stanley leaving Hudson's hands and his fragile skull colliding with the cement slab the universe went silent and time stood still.

As the doctor's body dropped to the ground like a sack of old newspapers, Hudson's gaze moved to the dome's computer station that was flickering to life and beyond it to the bizarre nothingness that was violating the universe's force of survival outside of the dome.

He looked outside of his plastic fortress and into the doctor's laboratory where ice manifested itself on everything. A mere moment later, the world outside the dome burst at once into a thousand fragments of nothing moving slowly through the air, dust of matter worthlessly falling to a swelling ground.

Hudson stepped to the dome, and tears filled his eyes he put his hands upon the glass but leapt back in pain from the burning sensation in his palms.

"Stanley..?" he whispered. He looked down to find the man lying on the floor where he'd dropped him, with his eyes glued to the computer display across the dome.

The processing speed was unbelievable. They both watched as sixteen data feeds came in and the computer began to process them automatically. Though the universe was already rebounding, the video began to process the actions before the Kelvin blast, and the actions before that led to those, and so on, playing full-spectrum video of time in reverse.

"Oh my gosh, Stanley. It's working. It's really working. How? It's too much data." Hudson's eyes were pinned to the computer screen and he began to move slowly towards it.

The old man didn't answer.

Hudson saw heaven and earth recede on each of the sixteen screens. He saw our own solar system crushed together from fragments that came from the universe beyond. The video sped up to show the lapse of billions of years in only seconds.

"Stanley, what does this mean?" Hudson asked as a blackness overtook the screen while the matter of the universe raced before his eyes.

"Stanley," he said louder. Still with no response. "Stanley!" he shouted now, arousing his anger once more. He turned to look behind him where the old man still lay. "What does this mean?"

But a pool of blood had formed around the old man's ear, and Dr. Stanley Hopewell was having trouble seeing his only friend now that he turned his vision from the computer monitors. He tried to move his arms so that he could right himself and stand up, but only his eyes turned to Hudson and his lower lip quivered just slightly.

Stanley's eyes looked beyond Hudson's imploring, concerned faced and saw the last few frames of the video pass away. "Oh, dear God..." Dr. Hopewell gasped.

"Stanley, what is it? Stanley..." Hudson bent down to shake the old man, to rouse the defiant, resilient bastard back to his genius when it was needed most of all.

"Fate..." was the last hypothesis of Dr. Stanley Hopewell, whose mind faded to blankness as he had seen the origins of the universe do just now before his eyes.

"Oh, God... oh, God no..." Hudson shouted as he jumped up. He ran to the cabinet and threw out the MREs looking for medical supplies or a miracle that might save the old man.

He kicked over the pile of boxes and threw open the tops, dumping them out on the ground and moving to the next until he'd gone through the lot.

Finally, exhausted, he came back to stand by the aged doctor's motionless body. Looking over at the prodigious pile of imperishable food and a few seeds that stood in a great heap, he fell to his knees beside his friend and buried his face in his hands.

Behind Hudson's shaking back the video looped to begin once more from the beginning, leaving the unknown to pass forth again and again.

Like the great dew upon the surface of the planet earth, Hudson's tears fell and spattered into tiny fragments of mist upon the cement slab beneath him.

APPRAISAL

By Brad Pauquette

Murray was younger than his name and mustache led his patrons to believe.

It was 2:01 in the morning, and, tired of yelling at the two drunks passed out on a table across the bar to wake up and go home, he stepped out from behind his oak prison to rouse them himself.

"You ain't gotta go home, but you can't stay here," he'd relished shouting the old cliche for the first two weeks on the job, in his South Boston accent that he'd amped up to win the gig. After three years of closing the bar Wednesday through Saturday all he wanted to say now was, "Seriously, get the hell out."

It'd been a slow night. He doubted there was eighty bucks in the tip jar, which he'd split with the girl that helped him clean up tables. Combined with his two dollars an hour, he'd be lucky to walk out with sixty bones to his name, and that was before the tax man took his toll.

But what could he do? It was a Wednesday.

"What a coupla' ass clowns..." he muttered to himself as he slalomed amongst the bar's cheap Formica tables to the one in the rear where these two gentlemen had made their last stand. "...I don't rememba' servin'em more'n two beers apiece, musta brought it with'em... ass clowns."

"Hey big fella," Murray shouted, placing his hand on the man's shoulder and shaking. "Bar's closed."

Getting no response, he moved to the thinner one and shook him harder than he had the last. "Wake up buddy, bar's closed."

The man slumped off of his stool, the weight of his lanky body dragging his chin off the table top to meet him on the floor.

There were three things that Murray was unaware of. He didn't know that the rhino slumped over the table like a bag of wet cement was named Hank, he didn't know that the skinny one piled on the floor like a soft pretzel was Larry, and until he bent down to check under Larry's jawbone for a pulse, he didn't know that they both were dead.

Hank and Larry had met each other exactly one year before when Larry had stopped by Hank's house to buy a used snowblower.

"Hey, this is Larry, I've been emailing you about the snowblower you listed on Craigslist," he introduced himself to Hank over the phone. "I'm in the neighborhood now, you mind if I stop by and take a look?"

Five minutes later, which was five minutes earlier than promised, Larry placed his briefcase underneath the passenger seat and hopped out of the car, ambling through the cold to Hank's doorstep.

119 thousand, he thought to himself as he made his way up the walk. *2,500 square feet, single car garage. Semi-suburbs, city schools, 127 if it had a finished basement.*

He rapped confidently on the glass storm door and smiled, trying to pass his best "just here for a snowblower" look through the peep hole. The sharp January wind stung his cheeks and wrists as he waited, but failed to pierce his large down jacket. An inflated jacket might make some men look more strapping, but not Larry, the juxtaposition of his skinny corduroy clad chicken legs sticking out of the massive coat made him look more like a cartoon character than a threat.

Showing up early was a rule of Larry's—show up close

enough to on-time to not be out of the ordinary, but early enough to throw things off balance.

Hank had rules of his own. He peered out at Larry from the bedroom window upstairs and let him ring the doorbell a couple of times.

"You must be Larry," Hank said, opening the door just as Larry was pulling out his cell phone to call and confirm the appointment. Hank stood in the doorway and seemed to Larry to occupy the entire frame of it. His scruffy blonde beard met the thermal Henley that covered the chest hair partially exposed by the two open buttons on Hank's flannel shirt. Hank looked like a plumber to Larry, but he couldn't imagine the bulky man squeezing his girth into the cabinet underneath of a vanity sink.

"Yeah, still got that snowblower?"

"Come on in," Hank told him cordially, with a trusting grin. "It's freezing out there today."

"No kidding." Larry shivered theatrically. "I've been in the car for a bit running errands. You mind if I use your bathroom real quick?"

Perfect, Hank thought. "Yeah, no problem, right this way."

Perfect, Larry thought to himself and grinned as he followed the big man to the first floor bathroom.

From the looks of the primary hallway, Hank, or probably his wife, had hit the sponge painting fad hard in the late 90s. No stucco? No problem, try a splotchy paint job instead. *Maybe 115*, he thought.

The two story house was laid out in the typical suburban style with dining room, living room and kitchen joined together with half walls, and a stairwell in the center that split the first floor in two. Upstairs, Larry knew that later he'd find two bedrooms to the left of the stairs and two to the right, with a bathroom in the middle.

"Here it is," Hank told him, gesturing towards the far end of the hallway. "I'll be in the kitchen."

Larry smiled to himself as he closed the door behind him. "Such a friendly fellow," he muttered as he turned to the toilet and, leaving his gloves on, prepared to relieve himself—best to keep up appearances in case anyone was listening.

He smiled and enjoyed the relaxing, easy-going feeling, then zipped back up and turned on the sink water. He reached into his pocket, removed the Taser he brought into the house with him, and flipped off the safety. He always wished the weapon would hum with power, so he substituted the sound with his own melodic hummmm.

Larry turned off the water and grasped the door handle, exhaling like a body builder straining on the weight bench.

Slowly but with purpose, Larry opened the door, wrenching the handle all the way past him with his skinny arm.

"Hank, you there?" he blindly called into the open hallway from the safety of the bathroom doorway.

Heavy footsteps approached from the opposite direction he'd expected.

It's ironic that the brain of a self-obsessed, intelligent species can both speak and listen at the same time. At that moment, Larry stepped into the hallway with his downcast profile to Hank. As he lifted his gaze to meet the approaching man he heard himself say with the deadpan tone of an action movie villain, "Perhaps I'll sell your soul on Craigslist," *and* heard a gruff voice surprisingly dissimilar to the cordial voice he'd heard on the phone say "Say hello to the Craigslist Killer..."

Hank froze where he was and Larry nearly dropped

his Taser to the floor. Larry's eyes squinted in shrouded bewilderment.

"What did you just call yourself?" Larry demanded, turning his body to square his shoulders towards the hulking man who had stopped 12 feet down the hallway. Hank also held a live Taser in his right hand. His face wore the shadowy remains of a sinister grin that had turned to confused anger like the face of a grizzly bear forced to play Soduko.

"Did you just say that you're going to 'sell my soul on Craigslist'?" Hank asked, turning up the last words to emphasize his mockery.

"I said what I said..." Larry stopped, failing to find another word to follow the last, expending all of his mental energy mustering an intimidating look into his awe-struck face.

"What a lame line, seriously..." Hank told him. "Did you stay up late last night thinking of such a terribly clever thing to say?"

"You are not the Craigslist Killer," Hank continued, peppering his voice with the playful hatred in his eyes. "Don't fool yourself little guy, there can only be one."

"We'll see," Larry said, and he raised his Taser to eye level.

Unfortunately for Larry, Hank shared exactly the same impulses. Imagining himself in a western gunfight, Hank raised his Taser in exact synchronization with Larry. As soon as the other man's chest was in the center of the sites, both men's brains sent electrical impulses away from the brain and down the arm, contracting the finger around the Taser's trigger. In the slow motion that accompanies adrenaline-pumped, near-death experiences, Larry saw his electrical stingers pass by Hank's in midair exactly halfway down the hallway. The glory of his direct hit to Hank's chest was dampened by the barb that pierced his own down jacket in his right breast, and smothered by the second barb that slipped between the open coat buttons to strike just above his navel.

50,000 volts of electricity passed from each man's Taser to the other man's body. Larry's muscles contracted in spasmodic waves and he collapsed to the floor. Though the reaction took longer to overtake his brawny body, Hank followed suit and fell face down to the carpet.

Both men wriggled like earth worms frying on a hot sidewalk. The spasms, which couldn't accurately be described as pain, would cease for a moment, but begin again as soon as the victim caught his breath.

For several minutes, both men writhed in convulsions. Amidst the uncomfortable tightening and release of muscle mass, each was left in silence to his own thoughts.

"Hey Hank." Larry called out between tyrant pulses of electricity terrorizing his nervous system.

"Yeah?" came the agonized reply.

"What if we don't kill each other?"

There was a long pause as Hank thought, the right side of his body twitching in waves from his abdomen up through his shoulder and down to his elbow.

"Either one of us cou..." Larry's face froze and his jaw thrust forward uncontrollably, "could get up first."

Hank's buttocks were twitching, and when he'd tasered himself before this was a sign that it was almost over. But nonetheless, Larry made a good point, and Hank had never been a fan of competitive sports.

A palpable silence hung over them, and a peace invaded the twitching room.

When the impulses had finally retreated from his buttocks to tickle his toes, Hank asked "What line of work are you in?"

Larry took his time considering Hank's question, which was as much a proposal. "I appraise real estate," he ultimately responded, "...you?"

An hour later they were sitting at Hank's kitchen table while Larry nursed a glass of water.

"I've got to say, you look really unimposing when you stand at the front door," Hank complimented him.

"Well you, sir, have a fantastically mellow phone voice. I thought this was going to be too easy. I almost didn't come!"

Thus their whirlwind bromance began. First it was a beer or two once a week, and the occasional movie. Both knew to talk about their hobby would be reckless, but it was the idea of kindred honesty and openness, existing nakedly without judgment that was so satisfying.

Larry met Hank regularly about town. By February, they had lunch at Panera routinely and coordinated a weekly schedule of happy hours that rarely faltered.

Enjoying the excitement of his new friendship and having determined that his methods merited review, Larry took a sabbatical from his pernicious hobby. In any case, he barely had time to run the proper prep-work.

But in March, Larry was ready to get back in the game. He parked his car along a suburban street just north of town at 2:20 p.m. for a 2:30 appointment he'd scheduled by email to take a look at a used scroll saw.

He parked his car in front of the brick ranch and surveyed his victim's home. It had been several months since Larry had successfully taken a victim, but he didn't feel rusty, he felt energized—like a distance runner after a day off.

Let's see, single story ranch. But brick, nice suburb. One hundred... Head in the game, Larry! Head in the game, he rebuked himself.

Walking to the door, he reached into the pocket of his long, black trench coat and flipped off the safety on his Taser. Drama provided opportunity for failure.

Larry knocked and then he waited. Then he rang the door bell and waited some more. Finally, the door cracked and a shadowed face and bulging eyeball appeared just above the security chain.

"Larry?" a timid voice of a big man asked. Larry peered into the darkness to read the eye that watched him.

"Hank?" Larry asked, and the silence confirmed the answer. "Hank? What are you doing here?"

"Uhhh...," Hank stammered, "selling a scroll saw. Want to come in I guess?"

"No, not really...," Larry was astounded, not knowing whether to rage or chuckle. "What are you doing here? This isn't your house."

"No, I know. I'm just watching it," Hank told him. Through the cracked door, he confessed that the house they'd met in hadn't been his either, he'd just been house-sitting.

Confused and dejected, Larry shook his head at the poorly-constructed explanation of Hank's position and returned to his car. He sat and stared at his steering wheel, as if the leather-grained vinyl might offer some philosophical insight.

Two minutes later Larry drove away without knowing who was more stupid. Surely, it must have been stupidity on someone's part. Of course, it's only natural, Larry and Hank staged themselves to be the perfect buyer and seller.

APPRAISAL • *Brad Pauquette*

Larry didn't call Hank for five days. When he did, neither of them mentioned the incident or the absence.

Despite their persistent friendship, a kind of melancholy set over Larry. He considered that fate might be sending him a message about his past time, or perhaps he wasn't as good at his hobby as he'd always imagined and it was time to move on. In any case, Hank often bought the first round of beer.

It wasn't until September that Larry was willing to try again. In rebounded spirits, he searched carefully for the perfect Craigslist ad. *Maybe someone giving away a cat*, he thought. No, the stereotypes weren't strong enough to be reliable. Perhaps, he could hire a baby sitter—but it was safer to make a house call.

Finally, he found the perfect advertisement. "Used Twin Mattress. Must carry down stairs from efficiency high-rise apartment. I can help, but you might want to bring a friend. Only used for three months while here on extended business, must sell by Saturday."

An apartment building isn't ideal, pesky neighbors to overhear, but that risk was more than balanced with the other details.

"Price sounds great" he emailed, tapping his keyboard excitedly. "Can come right away."

Ninety minutes later he was happily bouncing out towards his pickup truck in a hooded sweatshirt with a spring in his step. He parked his truck outside of the building, plucked a few coins into the meter to the tune of "I Love the Flower Girl" and bounced up the stairs to the ninth floor.

Standing in front of the door to 914, he carefully placed a congenial smile on his lips, looked endearingly into the peephole and rapped on the door in a playful rhythm.

There was no movement behind the door while he counted to ten, so he knocked again.

God, please no, he thought to himself, hidden behind the smile. He prayed silently as he knocked the third time.

Finally came the motion of something big behind the cheap, hollow-core door. A silent, "Christ," echoed through the plywood and veneer.

"Hank, it's you, isn't it," Larry called out.

"Yeah, Larry, it's me," came the hesitant, defeated reply.

Without another word, Larry turned and left, walking briskly with his shoulders down and lips moving with a steady stream of curses.

Popping into his truck, Larry again sat and asked his steering wheel for guidance. He'd put 45 minutes in the meter, and he'd be damned if the city was going to steal those quarters from him.

Larry jumped when he looked over and saw a big, wet face outside of his passenger side window. Hank was standing there in his typical outfit, complete with flannel shirt and jeans, begging Larry to put the window down.

"I'm sorry," Hank sobbed. "I don't know why this keeps happening."

Larry didn't even look him in the eye.

"Maybe we can work out some sort of system," Hank continued. "Like a code-phrase in the ads, or maybe we can just give each other a black-out date or something."

"That's the dumbest thing I've ever heard," Larry snapped. "How do you even find these houses?"

"Craigslist... house-sitting..." came the fragile reply.

"How do you not get caught?! You have got to be the stupidest son-of-a-bitch alive!" Larry chastised the big, weeping man who stood with his forehead against the truck's door frame.

"Here's our system," Larry told him between the giant's sobs. "Next time this happens, I'm going to do what I came to do. I will kill you."

The tires screeched as the truck peeled from its position. In his rear-view mirror, Larry saw Hank spin around and fall to the ground.

By the time Larry arrived home, he knew he had done something terrible. As best he could identify, he felt something between heartburn and nausea welling inside of him.

He called Hank's cell phone, but no one answered. He hung up without leaving a message.

He said he'd wait an hour and try again, but after 20 minutes he slowly dialed the numbers. Still no answer.

This time he left a message for the only man whom he called a friend. "I'm really sorry, Hank. That was stupid. I was just frustrated. Please call me."

For a week, each day he'd call. "Please call me," he ended each message. Then he stopped. Two days passed, then three.

The following Saturday, Hank's number flashed across Larry's caller ID. Larry's hand darted for the phone, but then he found himself watching the number flash across the screen for two rings, four rings. Hank didn't leave a voicemail.

Larry's life took a turn after what he began to refer to in his mind as "The September Affair".

Following that bleak, conflicted Saturday, things spiraled around Larry as if his apathy had hands. Some weeks his coworkers at the real estate appraiser's office would discuss the great number of hours he was putting into his job, other times they'd huddle up and ask "where the hell's Larry?" and "I haven't seem him in days." "I hope he's OK," they would lie.

Some weeks his home appraisals would be too high, and the bank would request a second opinion. On his absent weeks, he valued them 20% below the loan amount without ever setting foot in the neighborhood.

By mid-November, Larry found himself browsing the hardware store a couple of nights each week without knowing why. One Wednesday he spent 45 minutes staring at the selection of ropes, though he already owned several. The following Monday he found himself standing in the pest control aisle, though his mind was filled with a peculiar interest in how much weight a residential garage rafter would support.

Just curious about the price, he told himself, *never know when that information might come in handy. Isn't rat poison just more mouse poison? Why's it so much more expensive?*

In December, he saw a pharmaceutical commercial that helped him identify the symptoms of depression, so he began to keep a journal. It wasn't a journal with dates and feelings on the days goings-on, but more like a compilation of his life's events, strung together as if they might reach a conclusion. *A lot of people get depressed around the holidays*, he thought. *Writing is good for the soul. Besides, if something happened...* but he never allowed himself to finish the thought.

His writing didn't cure his depression, but it did inspire him to visit some of the things he enjoyed as a child.

He spent a Tuesday morning at the science museum, re-exploring the exhibit on the human body, and single-handedly lifted an entire car with the weight of his body and a simple lever. He was supposed to be appraising a home in some pseudo-suburb a hell's commute from the city center.

Value's determined by the market, anyway. If somebody's

willing to pay it, that's what its worth. This isn't communist China, he rationalized while watching a video about supernovas in far space.

On the way home, he saw a billboard for an indoor water-park. *Now that's luxury, I should take a day off after Christmas. A Christmas will be nice*, he lied to himself, and in a sub-tier of his brain counted the great number of movies that end happily at Christmas.

Christmas came and went. Larry saw his brother's family for long enough to despise them for being loud and commercial-laden fools. He went home and began watching *It's a Wonderful Life* on TV, but turned it off when George Bailey jumped into the river.

The Tuesday after Christmas, Larry stood in line for a slide at an indoor water park just outside of the outer belt. He was in the back of the line, with 20 minutes between himself and the wooden stairs. He hummed and considered the way his navel sunk into the small pouch of fat on his abdomen, a flaw he'd worked for years to fix but finally gave up when he turned 40.

As he moved on to consider the asymmetry of his toes, he heard a familiar voice step into line behind him.

"Come on, Brian, we'll do this one first then we'll get a pretzel. It's Stacy's turn to pick," the gruff, but cordial voice reached his ears.

"Please? You guys can stay here, I'll be fine," came the whiny voice of a nine-year-old boy.

"No way. Everybody stays together, we promised your mom. There's a lot of creeps out there."

Larry spun around to find himself looking at the back of a man who stood in his bathing suit like a billboard covered with flesh.

"Hank?" Larry timidly inquired to the broad shoulders in front of him.

Hank turned from the bartering session with his wards to meet Larry's eye.

"Larry? I'll be damned! What are you doing here?" he shouted and opened his arms as if to step in for a hug, but stopped short, returning his hands to his sides and placing his palms flat against his thighs.

"Standing in lines, mostly. I didn't... I didn't know you had kids."

"Oh, these brats? No, I'm just watching them over Christmas break. I could use the cash."

"How the hell did you pull that off?" Larry asked, aghast that anyone would permit Hank to watch their kids, further—pay him. But he knew the answer before the words left his mouth.

"Craigslist." Hank confirmed with a grin and a wink.

"Jesus, Hank, you're not..." Larry knew he couldn't stop the horror from assaulting his face, "you're not..."

"Oh, no! No way!" Hank insisted, spreading his hands in innocence. "God, no... I just needed the money, really."

"Thank God," Larry said, expelling air like a popped balloon.

Their conversation fell short, and Larry returned to consider the consequences of symmetry and podiatry.

Hank chewed on his lower lip as he surveyed the area for at least a minute and a half. "You want to get a pretzel or something?" he asked Larry.

Much to young Stacy's disappointment, two minutes later she and her brother were sitting at an adjacent table enjoying a soft pretzel while Larry and Hank pieced their way through a conversation.

"So... have you?" Larry finally asked, breaching the single unspoken rule of their former friendship.

Hank just shook his head, and took a big bite of his pretzel. "You?" he said through a doughy glob.

"Haven't found myself in the mood," Larry admitted. "I felt so bad about everything. I'm so sorry Hank. I acted like a real ass."

"It's really okay, man." Hank paused. "I mean you were right, it just couldn't work. It'd be stupid to try."

Larry waited, and carefully chose his next words. "You can have it..."

"Have what?"

"You know... 'It', I think I'm out."

Hank's eyes widened in an emotion bred by surprise and concern.

"You don't have to do that," Hank said. "Don't put that on me."

"No, I mean it. Maybe I'm not cut out for it," Larry elaborated. "Maybe we should just hang out a few times and figure it out... you know, I can be out, it's okay."

"You mean it? I mean, I could be out too... it's not like I'm really 'in' right now anyway."

"No, I want you to be in it," Larry insisted. "You've got something here that I don't," Larry admitted, motioning towards the kids. "I can't do it the way you can do it."

"You know what, Larry," Hank said after a contemplative pause. "We'll figure it out. Let's figure it out."

After a long day at the water park, the awkward conversation spawned by time lapse was defeated and the old Hank and Larry were back. Larry climbed into his bed that night happily exhausted from the cold water, grinning as he drifted into sleep.

Two weeks later Larry and Hank stepped out of a blustery January evening, a Wednesday, into the warm wooden embrace of a bar neither of them had ever visited before.

They chose a table near the back, and looked out over the dive's few patrons on this lonely night. They talked about the bartender whose thick mustache didn't seem to match his lean body and unwrinkled face, leaving him an ageless spectacle.

Murray, the bartender, introduced himself when he delivered a second round before they asked. Larry used the bathroom while Hank drained the remainder of his first beer, and a few minutes later Hank followed suit.

When Hank returned to the table, Larry seemed oddly contemplative. Hank forced himself to continue their commentary on the eccentric weeknight bar goers, but it wasn't two minutes before his speech faltered and he fell silent.

"Larry, I've got to tell you something," Hank said after a long, silent pause that sank heavily over the table.

Larry's blue eyes, set close together in his narrow face, were filled with a sweet sadness. He turned to his prodigal friend. "Yeah?" he said, turning up the corner of his mouth in a compassionate smile.

"I'm sorry, Larry, but I poisoned you," Hank weakly told his skinny friend sitting on his left.

"I know," Larry said with an uncommon understanding and sympathy in his voice. "I tasted it a few minutes ago."

They both looked at their half-drunken beers.

"I poisoned you, too," Larry told Hank, looking up into his great brown eyes. "But it was before I knew that you poisoned me."

"I know," Hank said, and a tear rolled down his cheek. Larry raised his glass, and Hank followed suit.

"For what it's worth," Hank toasted solemnly, "my only friend." A dampened clank rang out over the bar, and the two drained their glasses. They shook hands and looked into the eyes of each other, recognizing their reciprocal trust.

Then each resigned himself to watch the last remnants of foam slip to the bottom of the glass while they considered this final toast. As the bubbles pooled into liquid, their heads slipped together to the table and each drifted into peaceful contemplation.

"Every penny," Larry slurred past his tongue. Hank offered no response, even if he had, Larry's eyes had slipped closed and his mind was released into eternal slumber before the words had yet glided past his lips.

Two hours later, Murray was kneeling down with his hands under Larry's jawbone.

"Jesus priest, Sandra, this guy's dead," he shouted across the bar. Moving to the big brute still sitting at the table, "oh shit, the big one is dead too!"

Murray ran back to his fortress behind the bar and snatched the phone from its hold.

Acknowledgements

Columbus Creative Cooperative would like to thank all of the individuals and organizations that made this book possible. It was, without question, the product of many hands.

Thank you to the following founding executive members of Columbus Creative Cooperative. Your insight into each other's work and spirit of collaboration is invaluable:

Amy Dalrymple   Matt Hance
Chad Jones   Paige McCorkle
Ben Orlando   Brad Pauquette
Kim Younkin

Thank you to the following local businesses that generously sponsored our material:

Gretel's Handcrafted Soap (GretelsHandcraftedSoap.com)
Le Pooch (LePooch.net)
Lexi's on Third (LexisOnThird.com)
Melissa Pauquette Photography (MelissaPauquettePhotography.com)
Sunny Meadows Flower Farm (OurSunnyMeadows.com)
Tracy A. Younkin, Esq. (Bankruptcy-Attorney-Ohio.com)

Thank you to our editors, Brad Pauquette and Kim Younkin, and a special thanks to Mallory Baker, for her superb proofreading.

Finally, thank you, dear reader, for appreciating and supporting local art. With the help of generous patrons like you, Columbus Creative Cooperative can continue to educate and encourage local writers, support local businesses and entertain the fantastic readers of Ohio.

For more information about Columbus Creative Cooperative, please visit **ColumbusCoop.org**.

Sunny Meadows Flower Farm is a proud sponsor of
Columbus Creative Cooperative's anthology *Origins*.